"Nooo!" he heard Julep shout, then the woman echoed at him while he gained his feet. Slocum ran toward the struggling pair, a welter of flailing legs, dust, grunting, and screaming. They were too intertwined for him to shoot safely, so he jammed the Navy into his holster and dove onto what looked like the back of a young Apache.

Immediately the man bucked like a bronco and his sweaty skin proved tough to hang on to, but Slocum managed to slip an arm around the brute's neck. Biting teeth and the clawing fingers of one hand lashed at him, stinging and drawing blood. Slocum felt it well on his skin, and it ignited a dormant urge to shake off the binding wraps of infirmity that had tightened about him for weeks since his unexpected drop into the canyon.

With a mighty bellow of rage, Slocum yanked hard backward, felt things inside the young man's neck tightening, then slowly giving way to his crushing choke hold.

JAKE LOGAN

SLOCUM
AND THE REBEL
CANYON RAIDERS

THE BERKLEY PUBLISHING GROUP
Published by the Penguin Group
Penguin Group (USA) LLC
375 Hudson Street, New York, New York 10014

USA • Canada • UK • Ireland • Australia • New Zealand • India • South Africa • China

penguin.com

A Penguin Random House Company

SLOCUM AND THE REBEL CANYON RAIDERS

A Jove Book / published by arrangement with the author

For information, address: The Berkley Publishing Group,
a division of Penguin Group (USA) LLC,
375 Hudson Street, New York, New York 10014.

ISBN: 978-0-515-15440-5

PUBLISHING HISTORY
Jove mass-market edition / May 2014

PRINTED IN THE UNITED STATES OF AMERICA

10 9 8 7 6 5 4 3 2 1

Cover illustration by Sergio Giovine.

1

Slocum felt the hot breath on his face before he opened his eyes. Even in his half sleep, he knew that while there was potential danger, there was also ample reward. And as he lazily raised his eyelids, like a sun-baked Gila monster disturbed by a redtailed hawk's shadow, Slocum felt the grip of the savage young thing's bold, firm hand tightening on him, none too gently, willing him to life.

Raw, new sunlight squinted Slocum's eyes and hazed a blazing silhouette around the dark girl's head, not unlike a halo, though this she-devil, he knew, was anything but holy. As his eyes adjusted to the light, he made out the sharp features of her face—the long, slender nose ending in a near-point, nostrils flared proudly at the base.

Her eyes were as dark as her hair—inkwell black with a far-off glinting, like the promise of a diamond, in the center of each. The full bottom lip, firm and sensual, was topped with a thin lip curving into a sneer of disdain and temptation all at once. She had worn that same look when she'd gotten the drop on him, bold as brass, the evening before.

He figured she had to have been watching him, waiting

him out. He'd not heard nor felt a thing that might have warned him he was not as alone at the little oasis as he thought he had been. It wasn't until he'd picketed the Appaloosa and shucked his trail-dusted duds that he'd sunk into the hot spring.

He'd kept his Colt Navy close at hand, but the bone-deep soaking heat had put him off his guard. He must have dozed— completely unlike him, especially him being a wanted man and all, cursed to ride the trails of the West, always with one long eye cast over his shoulder at his back trail, lest he should spy a law dog drawing close, waving a six-gun in one hand and a paper on him in the other. All for a self-defense shooting. But the man had been a judge, and Slocum had been a young, impetuous ex-soldier, unable to see past the theft of his family's farm in Calhoun County, Georgia.

Since then he'd been on the run, hoping that with every passing day he'd be forgotten by the law and left to live on his own, free of their watchful ways. But he didn't believe for one minute that would ever happen. So he led a cautious life, yet not so much so that he denied himself certain pleasures as they occurred. And there had been a few over the years. Few as zesty, however, as this Apache woman's bold ways.

He remembered the savage attack he'd endured the night before at her hands—and mouth. The slender young thing was anything but frail, though. She'd unleashed what seemed to him a lifetime of pent-up desire in a single, hour-long flurry of biting, thrashing, growling, pinching, and slamming that left Slocum nearly as worn out as if he'd spent two months riding drag on a trail drive to hell. Nearly.

Fortunately he was no stranger to giving as good as he got. And that was just what he did, matching her ministrations growl for growl, buck for buck, until they literally collapsed and fell apart, beyond breathless, so slick with a sheen of sweat they'd slid from each other like two halves of a length of seasoned, ax-split firewood.

And now here she was again, barely light out, and gripping him as if what he knew was about to happen didn't happen soon, she might just up and die on him. She didn't speak just yet, merely grunted, and with surprisingly firm hands, she jerked him sideways with one hand while the other, firm but smooth and experienced, worked him harder. That finally cleared away the last of the cobwebs of sleep from his mind. He returned the sneer and grunts, and with a quick movement, he spun her onto her naked back and plunged in for a good-morning gallop.

They'd begun to build up a long, slow head of steam, apparently just the way the girl liked it, for her sneer turned to a wide, lioness smile. She let her head drop back to the blanket and flop to one side, satisfaction threatening to make her really smile as Slocum tickled her depths. Her eyelids were the ones now to flutter, barely opening, as soft grunts rose up from her mouth.

Slocum rode her long, slow, and hard, her hips bookending his, her heels bouncing out of time against his lower back. Something about this young woman intrigued him so. He couldn't keep his eyes closed, couldn't look away from her face. And as he worked and watched her, those dark eyes snapped open wide. And with them, her slow gyrations and deep-throated purrings ceased.

He'd heard it, too. Sounded to him like a far-off coyote bark. But not to her.

The she-lion smile was gone, her gaze alert, yet focused on nothing, her body had stilled and gone rigid. He knew the signs of warning, of imminent danger, had seen them often in wild beasts. He, too, had developed a second skin of sense since taking to the trail years before.

And Slocum, too, now felt the inexplicable tingling that always began far back in his head and seemed to spread throughout his body within seconds. Something was not right. It bothered him not a little that she had sensed it before him, but he knew that as a full-blood Apache, she was far more in touch with her natural surroundings than he ever could be.

He knew enough about Apache to know that when in their country, a coyote that was not a coyote was most likely an Apache. Slocum and the woman slid apart once more, this time soundlessly, and as Slocum crawled a hand toward his holster, he saw the woman slip a stag-handled dagger from the small pile of doeskin that was her dress. At that moment, they caught each other's eye. She raised a finger to her lips in warning, then cut her eyes northward, beyond the rise that shielded their little oasis from approach. As he rose to his knees, she leaned close and whispered in his ear, "Far off still, you go. I will stay."

Slocum shook his head. "No, no way, Princess. I'm not about to leave you here alone. Not when I can protect you."

"From what?" she said, canting her head to the side. Then she did something that surprised him. She smiled and winked. "The chief is . . . my father." Again, she smiled a mischievous grin.

Slocum muttered, "Oh boy."

"You should go now. He will not treat you well. But me, he cannot hurt me."

The humor and the danger of the situation collided all at once in Slocum's mind, and he didn't know for a split second whether to stifle a snort of laughter or bolt for his clothes. He did both. "Daddy's little girl, eh?" he whispered to her.

But his comment was met with a mildly confused look. He didn't think he needed to waste time explaining what he meant. But she was right. He'd seen Mexicans tortured by Apache, and from the sounds of the approaching hoofbeats, there were many Apache, and if they weren't yet on the warpath, they would be soon enough. He'd be lucky to escape with his life, let alone his horse and gear.

He'd never saddled the Appaloosa as fast as he had. He hadn't bothered to button his shirt, nor tie his saddlebags behind the cantle. He'd slung them over his shoulder. Then just before mounting up, he bent back to the sweet little Indian maiden, who had also dressed herself, and said, "Are you sure it's them? They'll treat you well? I'll stay if you aren't sure."

Again she smiled and winked. Then rubbed a hand quickly across his crotch. "They are my people. Believe me." He looked into her eyes and something there told him she knew of what she spoke, and that it would be wise of him to get while the getting was still marginally good.

"We will meet again, John Slocum. I know this much." She winked, and as he grazed a kiss off her lips, she spun him around and patted his ass like a schoolchild being sent away. He swung into the saddle and didn't have but seconds to wait for the first proof that he was not welcome at the hot spring.

An arrow sliced the air by his forearm, left a hole in his flapping, unbuttoned red-and-white-checked shirt. Slocum gritted his teeth, crouched low, and looked back over his shoulder. The girl stood defiant, hands on her hips, her knife sheathed at her side, looking from Slocum toward the fast-approaching man on horseback.

Despite the fact that he was relatively sure she had been telling the truth about this approaching crowd being her people, he couldn't quite shake the feeling that she might be wrong. What if she was? She would die soon, that's what, he told himself. Not pretty, but you've made your decision, Slocum, old buddy, no way to change that now.

One last glance back over his shoulder and he saw the rider gallop into view, cresting the short ridge above the hot spring. It was a man, the most rugged Apache he'd ever seen, broad of chest, and with a stark white shirt open to the belt. The white of the shirt glowed against the leathered cherry skin, glinting with sweat. The man's wide face was topped with a plum-colored kerchief tied around his head, from under which bounced gleaming hair, straight and black as a crow's wing. It reached the man's wide shoulders, but crept no longer than that.

He rode a pinto barebacked, his long legs encircling the horse's gut, and tugged hard on the hackamore as he slowed before the girl. But he'd caught her glance backward at Slocum and followed her sightline. The hard, grim face grew even grimmer, and an oath that didn't sound at all like "welcome to tea" bellowed from him. He raised his right arm high and the rifle clasped in his fist cut the air like a swung ax.

And then a line of riders topped the rise to either side of the impressive man. Below him the young woman still stood, defiant and straight, only now she faced the man before her—Slocum assumed it was her father—and beyond, the line of warriors, her arms crossed over her chest.

It seemed she could take care of herself. And he'd better begin to worry about taking care of himself, or he'd not live to dally with another such fine young woman. He doubted there was another such as herself, in fact.

As Slocum broke from the dwindling line of runty mesquite at the base of the draw, before him stretched a long, barren plain with barely any ripples indicating rises he might use for cover. And the next second told him he wouldn't be needing them anyway.

Yips and howls from the human coyotes appearing on horseback to either side of him confirmed his fears. The broad-chested man had not been alone. Not by a long shot. There must have been eight or ten warriors approaching on either of Slocum's rear flanks. And they were closing in as fast as they could put heel to their mounts, yowling and yipping and loosing volleys of arrows, some of which overshot him, some of which pocked the earth just behind the lashing hooves of his bold Appaloosa.

He hoped no arrows would dimple his horse's hide. He liked the beast a whole lot and it would leave him afoot, surrounded by Apache. Unless the fall killed him. He tried to put out of his mind the mutilated, burned, gutted bodies of men, women, children, old Mexicans—it hadn't mattered to the Apache. They sought revenge for perceived slights not in kind but in blood. In hard, fast retribution that left nothing behind to question.

Slocum risked a look back, and shock tensed his shoulders, set his jaw, and forced him to heel his mount harder than ever, for the Apache were close enough that he had seen their rock-hewn features, all angles and fierce glinting stares from those dark eyes. The day before, he suspected he had ventured into the territory occupied by a band of Apache not known for its kindness to strangers, but he hadn't been sure.

All Slocum had wanted yesterday was to put a good bit of distance between himself and the overeager young law dog back in Minkville, the Colorado town he'd spent the better part of two months in before the newly elected deputy had decided to engage in a bit of hoeing out of the law offices.

Slocum had been tending bar in the Dilly Dollar when the young man had come in, talking with two other patrons about how he'd been going through all the old stacked dodgers when a couple had set off alarm bells in his head. They'd pealed warnings that told him for sure he'd seen at least a couple of those wanted men in his town. So he figured he just had to reconnoiter at the bar, have a cool beer, and when he went back to the office, he'd know who it was he'd see on the old posters.

Slocum had heard enough. And what's more, he knew the warning signs. Might be nothing would come of it, might just as well be that the lawman would dig a little too much in the dying past and come up with a dodger that told him John Slocum was a wanted man in his midst.

And so Slocum had reluctantly once more pulled up stakes and headed out. He'd intended to make it across the vast span of desert before another day had passed, but the two days' hard travel in the saddle had left him tuckered out—it had been many months since he'd had to spend long hours in the saddle. And the hot spring oasis had appeared as if it had sprouted and bubbled up out of the long, dry, cracked plain just for him.

And that was when he'd met the young Apache woman. It had been a bronc-stomping night of all-out fun. The woman knew what to do, and what she didn't, she made up for with a curiosity he'd rarely seen in a nubile young creature such as herself. The rambunctious proceedings had laid them both out as if they'd been staked and left to dry on the surrounding sandscape.

Another angry bee of a bullet buzzed too close by Slocum's fawn hat, and he slid his Colt Navy from its holster and thumbed it into action. He didn't really want to kill anyone, just warn them off, let them know that just because he was running from them didn't mean he didn't have a set of fangs and would rather strike than die on the run. Somehow despite the fact that he was the one being wrongly pursued, he couldn't help feeling guilty somehow, as if the Apache knew something he didn't.

As they pounded forward, pursued and pursuers, too many of the latter for Slocum's taste, time seemed to slow. Harsh chuffing rose up from his horse's powerful chest, the morning sun pulled wavering rays of heat off the fist-tight hardpack before him, and spider legs of sweat slipped down his forehead, collected in his eyebrows, and quivered there while he touched off another round over his shoulder. He swore he heard a yip cut short, strangle into a grunting gurgle, then the unmistakable sound of a man slapping hard to the unforgiving ground.

Slocum wished he felt something more than he did for the one he'd shot, probably killed. But he didn't. Too long he'd been pursued, too long he'd been overwhelmed by odds stacked too much in the house's favor. And this was just another one of those times. But those high rocks ahead would offer some shot at evening the odds, however slight.

Just like mountain ranges seen from far off, the pile felt more mirage than reality, as if he'd never reach it.

The sun continued its leeching ride skyward, baking everything beneath, pulling the strength from his horse. He felt the Appaloosa's strength wane, was amazed that it hadn't yet taken a shot from the Apache. Come to think of it, he should be more amazed that the Indians weren't shooting more. He risked another glance behind, and yes, they were still there, and had flanked him most effectively, making escape to either side impossible.

That told him a few things. First, that the Apache were in no rush to catch him. They must know something I don't, thought Slocum. And that something can't be good. The rocks rising up to form the cragged height ahead of him were his only hope, no matter what they represented. Beyond them he assumed was more of the same plain he now galloped over.

Another shot whistled by, far wide, and he knew then without a doubt that these Apache weren't after his hide . . . just yet. They wanted him alive. And since they had slacked off, though kept up their pursuit to the left, right, and rear, he knew what that represented—they felt sure they could trap him in the rocks.

Slocum guessed they were planning on circling the rocky knob, trapping him there, and waiting him out. It was obvious he had few supplies and his ammunition would be no match for theirs.

He would figure out those worries when he made it to the rocks.

And when he turned back around, patting the straining horse's lathered neck, the view beyond the rise of rocks began to inch into his sightline, up up up with each galloped step forward. And it revealed not more of the same desert plain he now traveled, but it was as if the earth dropped away, replaced with a remarkable vista both impressive and unnerving. Even the Appaloosa sensed what they were fast approaching and slowed his gait.

Slocum pivoted in the saddle—the Apache had also slowed. He swore he could see smiles on their faces. And no wonder, for the rocky rise before him, his last stop, formed the head of a hidden canyon.

Slocum swallowed back the hard knot formed of equal parts disbelief and queasiness lodged in his gorge. He'd worry about the canyon later. Right now he had to get himself and the Appaloosa into the rocks, secreted enough that he might pick off a few Apache before they got to him. If it seemed hopeless, he'd go out fighting. There was no way he was going to put up with torture for their sadistic pleasure. Torture his body all they wanted once he'd gone out fighting the bastards to the last, but he'd be damned if he was going to hand himself over to them without a hard-fought battle.

The sandstone seemed to reflect the heat off the very surface of a bacon-ready griddle. He felt sure if he spit on one of the rocks, it would sizzle and pop. Once behind a lower-down boulder, Slocum slipped from the saddle and slid out his Winchester rifle from its scabbard. Long-range work would require them to snipe him from a distance. It was worth the shot, even though they would work, he knew, to keep themselves back out of his range.

"Appy, old pal," said Slocum, stripping from his horse the saddle and blanket, and hastening to pour water into his cupped hands. He wasn't about to dump it into his hat. He'd seen a few decent hats ruined by such notions. He didn't think they were quite at that stage yet, though. "You're going to have to keep yourself hidden and low." Slocum realized what he was asking a horse to do and let out a short, tight laugh.

"I swear," he said, "if anyone were to hear me, they'd consider me officially around the far bend of the river. But right now, I don't much care." He patted the horse one last time, then led him into a narrow shadowed natural grotto of sorts.

He didn't expect there would be much use in trying to hobble or tether the creature—mostly because there were few places to do so—and where was the horse going to go anyway?

With the horse somewhat secure, Slocum reached back to the meager stack of goods he had in his possession. One saddle, a set of saddlebags half-filled with scant personal possessions, a blanket, and a small assortment of foodstuffs. That's all he owned in the world, and he didn't mind it one bit. But he sorely wished he had more food, a few more boxes of ammunition, maybe another water vessel or two.

But you don't, he told himself. Now get over it and snipe the foul yippers. Any notions he'd had minutes earlier of feeling guilty over killing one of them had long since vanished. Especially when he found out they knew they were running him toward the canyon. He had to climb deeper up and into the jagged tumbledown to get a better sense of the canyon. Maybe there was a steep trail down.

Up he climbed, looking for a toehold, keeping a watchful eye lest they had already surrounded him. He wasn't wholly convinced that they didn't want to just shoot him now, something they could do from a distance, instead of taking him alive, then torturing him. No thank you, ma'am.

Grit sprayed upward along the right side of his face, stung his eye. He ducked back down into the cleft in the rocks where he had just risen from. Another close shot followed that one. They had him pinpointed. He was only halfway up the rise, but already he knew he wouldn't stand much of a chance of getting all the way up. Opportunities for cover would dwindle the higher he might climb. He sighed and decided to make his way toward the back, the side of the knob he assumed overlooked the canyon.

One second, Slocum was inching his way around the backside of a particularly large boulder, keeping himself hunkered low and hidden, and the next, his right leg spasmed, stiff and trembling. He happened to have been looking downward when some Apache's lucky shot drove into his leg, spraying blood and meat up at his face. The bullet had threaded its way through the rocks, like a bee from hell, before finally finding a place to deliver its vicious dose of pain.

It slammed in just above his boot top, then out again a few inches below and behind his knee, taking what felt like a pound or more of flesh with it. The bullet spanged off the rock but didn't hit him again in its last gasp effort, before it dropped, spent in the grit of the declivity in which he found himself trapped.

Slocum's neck muscles tensed and he bit back the urge to bark an oath that would make a teamster blush. He scooched deeper into the narrow cleft, hoping it was enough to prevent him from being seen and shot again. Maybe they weren't interested in taking him alive, after all. Now he wasn't so sure that would be a good thing. Especially since he was wounded.

He'd been in many a tight spot before this, but now he knew he was really screwed. A lucky shot, that was all he needed. He didn't want to give the Apache the satisfaction or the upper hand that knowing he'd been shot might give them. Let them think he was just fine, holed up and waiting to pick them off, with any luck of his own, one by bloody one.

When the hot pain that clouded his senses began to diminish, Slocum pressed his temple tight to the cool shadowed rock and fumbled with the cotton bandanna he kept knotted about his neck, a regular and valued piece of his trail garb, especially useful when he found himself cutting through dry landscapes, kicking up the dust of the ages, swirling and choking everything in its path.

Once he'd knotted the thing as tight as he dared just below the knee, he flexed his leg. Felt like the bullet passed through. And it didn't feel like a big round, thankfully. Maybe he'd get out of this with nothing more than a limp. If he got out of it at all.

Blood had seeped into his boot, but he knew better than to shuck it, as the leg would swell and he might never get the boot back on again. But it did remind him to check his boot knife—still there. That little biter had come in handy more than a few times in his days on the trail, and he hoped it would for quite a while yet.

He let a few more moments pass, holding his breath, listening hard to the stillness. It seemed as if he could hear the very heat ticking from the rocks, the slightest of breezes soughing through the cracks and crevices. Finally satisfied that no one was scuffing their way closer, he sucked in a breath, snatched up the Winchester rifle from where he'd leaned it, and headed out past the big rock. He crept ever closer to the far side of the canyon, the overlook, hoping like heck he'd be able to find a perch from which to snipe the bastards, and if worse came to it, maybe he could find a way down. He hated to leave his horse and gear, but with any luck the Apache would give up and go home . . .

"Ha," he said as his head emerged from between two jag-ended boulders. And then the view before him took his breath away. It was truly stunning.

For a good half mile before him, the land dropped away hundreds of feet down to a canyon bottom that was cut lengthwise nearly through the middle. It looked from his birdlike vantage point to be divided by a stream switching back and forth. He also bet that on the ground, that stream would at least be a brook, maybe even something more substantial.

But the most interesting thing about what he was seeing way down there was the color green. He rubbed his begrimed, bloodstained fingers into his eyes and blinked hard. Yep, still green. He was seeing meadows and treetops. It was as if he were looking down on some sort of Garden of Eden. How could that be? Must be that waterway that nourished all that rich-looking landscape.

Surely the Apache knew of it. But what if they didn't? Or what if there was no way down there? Nah, the Apache had to be aware of it. Had to be. Maybe that was why they were chasing him so hard? Maybe they lived down there and they didn't want any whites to know about it? If that were the case, they surely wouldn't stop their attack. Maybe they were advancing on him from below, too. Great, he thought, Garden of Eden–dwelling Apache Indians from every angle.

How the vast vista before him had been hidden from view from every angle and direction he'd come from seemed almost impossible. And yet there it was, a genuine secret canyon. He scouted the rim with his eyes. It tapered to a narrowed end a good half mile away. But in between, the rim looked like any other canyon rim he'd seen. He wondered if riding on it from the east or west would look any different? Maybe it would appear to be an illusion until it was almost too late? He shuddered at the thought—a man at night on a hard gallop—hell, any sort of forward motion at all—might well take himself a tumble he'd never recover from.

And then a sizzling sound snapped him from his reverie. Something whipped by his head and he flinched. An arrow zipped right through the spot where his head had been, then sailed outward right over the little canyon and, losing its power, drifted downward. He lost sight of it as he watched, then jerked his head back—he didn't like the idea of getting killed just yet.

He looked left and right, and was rewarded with a narrow, flat, sandy ledge fronted with lower boulders forming a natural knee-high barrier between himself and open space over the canyon. Just behind him to the right, the rocks thickened and overhung the sandy ledge. This would provide him protection from above, a respite for a while at least from the sun. A little depression in the rock would allow him to take shots to his left and right without showing too much of himself. Problem was there wasn't much space for him to sit down and that shot leg was paining him something fierce.

He backed into the space and found it was deeper than

it had initially appeared—deep enough for him to ease down to a leaning position, enough so anyway to take the pressure off his bum leg. He sighed at the mild relief it gave him. He wished he'd thought to have filled his canteen the night before. It was a near-dry thing and so he hadn't bothered to take it with him after he'd watered the horse with a few meager cupped handfuls.

"Now we wait, Slocum old boy," he said aloud, still marveling at the sight before him, just mere feet away. He was looking down the length of the canyon, waiting for what might well be certain death. He couldn't go back, couldn't go forward, left and right would also be teeming with approaching Apache. He was screwed.

"Well, Slocum, you've been in tighter fixes, I'll say that. But this has to rate right up there with the best of them." He sighed again, slapped at the itchy little trail a drop of inching sweat made in the stubble on his face. "If you do have to check out, you had one hell of a last night." He almost smiled at the memory. But the throbbing in his leg and the picture in his mind of thousands of Apache crawling like lizards over the rocks toward him kept him from cracking a grin. His mind did like to make the most of a situation.

He double-checked the rifle, eased a shell into the chamber, did the same with his Colt Navy, and waited.

2

A mountain lion's low growl of warning stippled instant alarm across Slocum's shoulders and up his sunburned neck. He ground his teeth together hard and slowly squinted his right eye to squeeze a stinging runnel of sweat gathered there.

He'd gotten himself into a fine fix, caught between a shady overhang less than an arm's length to his left, under which he spied the dry, ribbed, wrist-thick girth of a coiled diamondback, and to his right, the soft scuffing sound of an angry-sounding mountain cat. Before him, the edge of a cliff and then hundreds of feet of open space, and behind, a creeping handful of pissed-off Apache.

And here he was in the middle, John Slocum, a bleeding wanted man with a long-term price on his head, no horse, his Colt Navy revolver with exactly two shells left, no hat to cover his baking head—he'd lost that while scurrying in the rocks moments before, trying to skedaddle away from the Apache's blood-seeking bullets—and a seeping wound in his left leg. He did have a small boot knife and a larger skinning knife sheathed on his belt. At the moment, they could do him no good. But in close-in fighting, they might be useful. And he had a feeling it would come to that soon.

Yessir, Slocum, he told himself. You're in a fine fix. With one useful leg, a snake that looked ready to strike if he shifted enough to deal with the padding approach of the lion, and the trailing Apache, who, if he rose up at all from his precarious haven in this cliff top tumbledown of rocks, would send a few bullets his way.

"Hellfire," he said, sighing. "This is no way to live, cowering in the corner and wishing you were somewhere else." He pulled in a deep draught of air and pushed himself to a standing position.

The lion poked its head out from between boulders to his right. From its size, it looked to be a she-lion, and she regarded him, an interloper on her mountain, with a cold stare, her ears pinned back hard to her head. In no time at all, she managed to slink forward, the thick whiskered snout bristling and stretching wide, a low-down growl guttering upward from her slowly stuttering chest.

Slocum didn't want a thing to do with her, but he knew it had gone far beyond that. He was committed to either being her next meal or killing her. And despite the fact that she could tear into him at any second, he felt no great inclination to end her days with a well-placed bullet. Not only would a gunshot tip off the Apache to his location, but he was, after all, a trespasser on her home ground. He bet himself a dollar that she had a den near there. And since it was still just past early spring, despite the heat, he figured she was protecting a youngster or two up there in the high rocks. That thought more than any other made him reluctant to kill her and leave her young to starve to death.

But the rattler to his left? Now that was another story. But how to dispatch that thick tongue flicker without giving away his location? Or without prodding the lion into death-dealing action.

As it turned out, the rattler didn't seem to have much

interest in Slocum. It had slithered into its spot just after Slocum had passed over the location himself. So once again he took stock of his situation, and found nothing had changed. He was still trapped by a viper, a lion, a band of angry Apache, and a drop of Lord knew how many feet straight down.

As the hours passed, the cat would disappear, then suddenly reappear as if conjured by a magician's hand. It was unnerving. The damn snake, however, just stayed right there, coiled like a living wad of massive rope. It had to be one of the biggest rattlers he'd come across in a long, long time, maybe ever. But as long as it stayed put, and so did he, Slocum reckoned they might both make it through the coming night without too many fang marks.

But it was the night that both nerved him up and gave him ideas. He had to do something, even if it was wrong. Soon his leg would swell tighter than a hat band on a fat man, he would dehydrate, and the Apache would swarm all over him like the angry bees they were. Then they could fight over his carcass—the snake, the lion, and the Apache.

Hey, wait just a cotton-pickin' minute, he thought. Wouldn't that be just the thing? Somehow play all these elements off one another, meanwhile, he'd be . . . gone. But how? He had hoped to use the coming nightfall to backtrack on out of there, slip back down to his horse, and ride hell-for-leather back across the plain.

He'd not heard a peep nor scuff of moccasin leather on rock since he'd gotten in this scrape, but he knew better than to trust that the Apache were gone. They were lurking somewhere close by.

Another hour dragged by. It became more of a chore for Slocum to rouse himself and fight his way out of the stupor and the increasing drowsiness that sickness from his wound and sunlight and lack of water was fast bringing him. And every time he did, and began to straighten up, maybe take a tentative inching step forward to cover the two feet to the cliff's edge before him, either the lion to his right or the damned snake—or both in concert—would hiss and growl. So they were waiting him out, too, eh?

As the purple hues of dusk deepened into near full dark, Slocum did his best to work feeling back into his numbing limbs, planning what to do in the next few minutes. For he knew that the Apache would make their move under cover of darkness. And that was any second. As if to confirm what he suspected, he heard the slightest of whisperings from somewhere above. If he hadn't been listening for it, he might well have mistaken it for a mouse foraging or a breeze rattling a dried stalk. But he knew better. The Apache were on the move.

He gripped his sheath knife in his left hand—ideal for slashing at the big rattler that he could just make out hadn't yet moved from its warm-rock spot—and in his right hand he kept the rifle at the ready. He could use it to thrust at the lion, and trigger it off should the need arise. Now the biggest challenge facing him was the low, natural escarpment just before him on the edge of the cliff.

Slocum shuffled forward, hearing just what he expected—the rattling and hissing to his left and a more insistent growl from the lion to his right. Too bad, they'd just have to live with it. But now the Apache would hear the noises and know where he was, and that he was on the move.

Time to leave. He managed to heft his wounded leg up on the rock, and glanced over at the snake. It was gone, not a surprise considering the sun had gone down and its cold-blooded self might seek the warmth of its den somewhere close by. The lion had moved forward, one bold step closer to him, her ears pressed flat to her wide skull. A slash of moonlight flecked her eyes.

And then two things happened at once: The cause of the whispering, scuffing sound from on high showed itself—skylined above were two Apache, the rounded heads, shoulders, and drawn weapons all rimmed against the purpling sky. And then, without warning, the cat leapt at Slocum.

His plan had been to tenderly explore the edge of the rim, scooting along it back toward the east, to his left, hopefully avoiding the snake, should it still be somewhere nearby, and then slipping back to the route he'd taken before to get back to his horse and gear. But the leaping cat and the poised Apache changed all that. Now he slipped over the rocks, maintaining a tight grip on them as his feet—one good one, one numb and throbbing—scrabbled for a ledge, a lip of rock, anything. What he found was less than promising. As his feet flailed, the wounded leg bumped and thrashed the same as its companion against the rock face.

He'd already sheathed his knife on his belt, and didn't have any easy way to secure the rifle, so he kept it gripped tightly, clunking it against the rock. The lioness's frustrated shriek told him she'd been barely deceived by his quick ploy. But a second later, Slocum felt hot breath choking in his face just before the big cat's mouth opened wide and lunged at his head. He gripped the rock tight with his left hand, and with his right, still gripping the rifle, he jammed it at her gaping maw as it drove straight at him.

Hot, razorlike pain flowered up his arm as his big knuckles collided with the cat's incisors. It bit down and thrashed left to right, but most of what it clamped on was gun stock and steel. Slocum felt the beast's teeth grind and snap, felt its blood mingle with his own as the great cat yowled and yanked on his hand and on the gun, not yet willing to give up the fight.

The cat's ire forced from it a rank scent of rage, much as a cornered creature will exude a stink of fear. Slocum drew back on the gun and rammed it forward and harder at the cat's thrashing mouth. Side to side the tawny-headed brute slashed, spittle flecking Slocum's face like rancid rain, her deep-throated screams cutting the otherwise still, clear night with raw rage and pain.

All the while, Slocum's trembling purchase on the rock

had begun to slip. His left hand had formed into a cramped claw that felt ready to snap apart at the slightest movement. His feet still found no edge, no slightly jutting wrinkle in the rock. His boots drummed and toe-scraped the rock face.

Would it be a sheer face, straight down to the bottom? All those hundreds of feet down? Would he be able to haul himself back up to the relative safety of the ledge before he dropped? He opted for that last thought, even as the she-lion whipped her head once more to the right, peeling the rifle from his grasp. The gunstock struck him a dizzying blow to the temple. He heard the weapon continue dropping, into the coming night, and below him, it clacked once against rock, then silence.

The now-familiar hot wetness of blood seeped into Slocum's right eye. Where was the cat? But he didn't have long to wait—for he heard it padding off, making an almost spitting sound, not yet comprehending the pain in its mouth. Never had meat fought back in such a way, Slocum was sure of it. But musing about the cat, which sounded as if it were stalking off toward its lair, would get him nowhere but dead. With a mighty heave, he flung his right arm upward toward the ledge he'd spent the previous hours on—and that was when the slight shadow fell on him. Slocum looked up into the leering face of an Apache warrior.

For a brief moment they merely stared at each other, then two more Indians appeared, flanking the first. They all moved closer, seeming, from their wide mouths and glinting eyes, to be enjoying his predicament.

The first, in the center, slipped a broad blade free from his belt and with no warning brought it down fast and hard at Slocum's outstretched right arm, which gripped the rock before him. His left was still gripping, barely, just below the rim, chin height to Slocum.

But he had to pivot and shift his weight to that hand, as well as to his chin—just in time, as the broad-bladed knife

flashed downward, slashing at the spot Slocum's hand had
been. The blade ground hard, ringing against stone, and the
bearer of the weapon howled a blue oath into the night air.

The three Apache moved as one—they grabbed for him,
but Slocum had swung his weight back onto his right hand
and chin, and with his freed left he risked its cramped state
to grasp his own hip knife. He freed it from the sheath and
swung it at the advancing three faces. From the shrieks
and the way they pulled back, he was sure the keen edge of
his blade found purchase in at least two of the three men's
chests and arms. It wasn't enough to buy him much time,
but he knew it would be a mere moment before the entire
ledge was filled with Apache ready to drill bullet holes into
his head, hands, arms, torso—anything they could see.

No, there was precious little way out of this up above.
But down below? Who knew? Maybe a ledge? It was rare
that a canyon wall didn't have some sort of crack, crevice,
or shelf. And then he felt strong hands grip his right, another
hand clasped tight about his left wrist, squeezing the already
rictuslike claw that was Slocum's left hand until in seconds
it proved completely helpless. His knife clattered against
stone.

They began hauling him up, dragging him back up over
the rocky lip to their waiting, hellish, torturous ways. This
would be a fate far worse than dropping to death into a canyon. Still, he vowed to fight them with every last twitch of
his body.

But something behind the Apache warriors had other
plans.

The close-up hair-raising howl of a lion is blood-chilling
at the best of times, but the shrieks of a wronged, enraged
she-lion, wounded, angry, and filled with an all-consuming
bloodlust incomprehensible to humans, seized all four struggling humans momentarily. For half a heartbeat, no one
moved, then all hell broke loose. The Apache let go their
hold on Slocum. His last vision in the near-dark above was

of a massive flailing form landing in the midst of the three shouting warriors. The yowling mother cat thrashed in all directions at once, dealing fang-and-claw fury veiled in a cloak of deafening rage that echoed far into the night.

As soon as the warriors let go of him, Slocum slammed back to the ledge, his chest hitting hard, and his legs and arms windmilling for purchase on anything at all. But they found none. He tumbled backward, still close to the rock. He sensed more than saw its massive presence to his left, felt air rushing by him, could see in his mind the hands of a clock slowing almost to a stop. Sound seemed to have pinched out, too. Then he hit.

His head bounced like a castanet against something much harder than a human skull, and his entire body sagged against it. But he was still conscious, awake, and aware. And what's more, the sounds and smells and sights missing moments before all rushed back to him.

Slocum lay there a moment, his head ringing and aching and clanging all at once, aware that he had hit a ledge, though how far he'd fallen he couldn't be sure. Wait . . . he heard something from above, a struggle—the cat and the Apache. So he couldn't have fallen all that far—maybe a dozen yards or so. But who knew. Who was winning up there? he wondered. He hoped it was the powerful she-lion. Though if other Apache showed up soon, she might well die. Even if she lived, they would probably hunt her and her cubs, knowing that they roamed the high rocky knob and made it their home—and knowing she may have taken the lives of some of their warriors.

He felt with his hands, patting the rock beneath him, at the same time awkwardly edging his right boot outward. He hadn't pushed it a few inches when his leg slipped off the rock. He almost pitched sideways from the shock.

"Easy, Slocum," he said in a voice he hardly heard. It sounded as if he were speaking underwater. He compensated by crabbing his left hand outward from his body, out along the rock, and it came to an abrupt stop mere inches from his hip. Could the ledge be that narrow? Could he be that lucky? Apparently so. How long was it?

It took most of his strength just to sit up. He edged as close as he dared to the cliff wall and his legs swung downward, the wounded limb throbbing anew. His legs' momentum almost pulled the rest of him with them. He stretched his left hand along the wall, felt the rock angle inward, and a vague flicker of hope let him think it might be a cave, a way into the rock face. Maybe even just big enough to crawl into and rest. He needed rest and time to think. He didn't even know if he had any weapons with him anymore.

The rocky wall continued to angle inward, still only mere inches, but it might prove enough to serve him well, if his luck held. But within another second, he knew this would not be the case.

The first strike barely surprised him. If it were not for the sound accompanying it, Slocum would have thought he'd bumped the back of his hand against a rocky spur. But it was no rock, and the sounds were distinct enough—and rapidly gained more than one voice. It was the unmistakable increasing din of a nest filled with disturbed, writhing rattle-snakes. And in the moonlight, as Slocum drew back his stricken left hand, already feeling odd, pulsing and throbbing with a strange pain, in the moonlight he saw a massive rattlesnake slide out of the small cave and stare at him.

And that was when he recognized it as the snake from the ledge earlier. Had to be. And just his luck as, with the lion, it, too, was a mama. A very protective mama. And she curved and writhed ever closer, hissing and rattling the entire way.

The second bite hit the same arm, but higher up, through his ragged shirt. At the same time, Slocum had been retreat-ing back to where he'd landed—mere inches away, but it was all the distance he had available to him. He saw the dull gleam of moonlight playing off the broad, thick girth of that mother snake—and she was coming straight for him. And followed by what looked like a dozen smaller versions of herself, all taking their time and heading toward nothing but him.

Funny, though, as he wasn't all that concerned. Instead he felt odd, sort of thick and buzzy, as if he were drunk and wrapped in gauzy bandages. Must be the viper poison filling up his body. He'd seen men die horrible deaths as they filled with the stuff and there was no way to help them . . . And now, Slocum guessed it was his turn.

Everything seemed lighter, brighter, and as he looked at the slowly advancing shapes, he realized he should try to stop them somehow. He thrust his boots at them, but it didn't seem to do any good, they just kept coming. He sensed he was near the end of his meager ledge, as he swung his right leg back up onto the narrow rock shelf, the big snake drove forward between his kicking boots, and with her wide, spadelike head raised up, she prepared to strike. The smaller forms slithered around her, under him, beside him, he felt them slide over his hands, press against his legs, one made its way up onto his belly . . . and that was when he ran out of ledge.

Slocum was vaguely aware that he was falling, and he knew he should be worried, knew that somehow this was it, the last of his days—and at night, too—but he felt only a thickening feeling, maybe something preventing him from breathing. He also was aware that something was on him, something that thrashed and flailed. Was it his own body? He didn't know, had a vague idea that it might be a snake, though why he wasn't sure.

And then, light and sound and feeling . . . everything just plain stopped.

3

The first thing he heard was a scream. Even before he opened his eyes, Slocum heard it. And it seemed to go on and on. Finally, he realized it was coming from his own mouth. Another voice joined his, but this one was smooth, low, soothing. He heard it for what seemed hours and eventually he realized that the other voice, his screaming voice, had stopped. But the soothing voice kept murmuring in his ear. What it said, he did not know, but it also did not seem to matter. Finally, though, he began to understand words in the soft murmuring, felt something touching him, a hand maybe, brushing his face, his arm, and feeling came back to him. But not much else. What was he doing here? And where was "here"?

". . . be okay, just relax now. You hear? Everything's gonna be just fine. Julep's going to make sure nothing else bad happens to you, you hear?"

Slocum let the words float in his mind. He chewed on them, worried the edges, then finally understood them. And to his surprise, when he thought about replying, he heard another voice, hoarse and barely more than a whisper, but it was a voice, and he thought that maybe it was his own.

"Where am I? What . . . what happened?" The act of speaking brought with it an unimaginable pain, as if talking had unlocked a door, and the room within was filled with sharp pains, dull aches, and splitting, slicing, searing agonies. His head throbbed, and his arms and legs felt as though they had been ripped off then nailed back on with steel pins driven by sledgehammers.

The soft voice sounded again, but he didn't understand what she was saying.

"Want to see . . . why can't I see?" he said through teeth gritted against the pain.

He heard the woman sigh, then she said, "I shouldn't. I covered your eyes because of your head bandage. Figured you might not be able to take the light just yet."

"Please. I need to see . . ."

She sighed again. "Okay then. But you got to keep your eyes as closed as you can for a while yet. Just peep a little bit, promise me that."

"Yeah, all right."

Slocum felt gentle hands tugging at what must have been the wrappings on his head. Why was his head bandaged? But he had no further time to muse on the subject, because a fresh round of throbbing pain washed over him as brightness invaded his eyes. It took him just as long to overcome the pain as it did to begin to make out dim shapes. He didn't speak for long minutes, and the woman, thankfully, didn't say a thing either.

Finally he was able to make out what the shapes were, then details, and lastly, just when he was about to say something, a face edged into view. He felt sure he had died and gone to his great reward. He'd long been unsure of just where he'd end up at the end of his days, his life being what it had been—a rough mix of good, bad, and ugly moments. But this creature staring down at him surely had to be an angel.

The light around her illumined her head from behind, but enough crept through and around her hair—golden hair at that—that he was able to see a kind, smiling face a few inches away from his. She had high cheekbones, a rounded face, a medium nose, not too sharp, nor too long, and full lips that rose in a smile.

"Are you . . . an angel?" he said in a croaking voice that had managed to come out barely above the previous whisper he'd emitted.

The angel giggled and shook her head. "I've been called a whole lot of things for a whole long time, mister, but I ain't never been called an angel." She leaned closer, laid a hand on his forehead. "I tell you, though," she said, preoccupied with tending to him. "A girl could get used to that sort of talk."

"How's the flying snake man?" A voice almost seemed to shout from beyond the woman.

She turned and said in a loud whisper, "Hush, you! He's come around and he don't need your big voice muddying up his head. Leastwise not yet . . ."

"Who's that?" said Slocum. He tried to raise himself up on his elbows, but the woman said, "Easy now. Take it easy there. That's just Deke. He don't do anything quiet."

"She's right," said the big voice, but beside him now. "Julep's right about most things. Like you, for instance. I swore you were a goner, but she told me to get on out and leave her alone. Said she'd fix you up, and by gum if she didn't. Though with a fall like that, and snakebit and shot and all . . ."

The words the man spoke rattled through Slocum like a series of hard punches to his chest. It was like watching a speeding train whip by, and every window was filled with a picture of something that had happened to him that day. Within seconds he remembered it all, from waking up at the hot spring with the beautiful Apache maiden, the one he'd called "Princess," then the chase across the plain, the

Apache hot on his heels, his Appaloosa pounding hell-for-leather toward that rock pile, that damned knob of high rocks.

He remembered leaving the horse, his gear, crouching low, skittering in between boulders, getting shot in the leg, the sun, reaching a place at the back near the top, seeing the vast hidden canyon stretching out far below, waiting, watching, the she-lion, the rattlesnake, so fat, so large, then the Apache attacking, going over the edge, landing on another ledge not far below, groping in the dark . . . snakes! All of it barreled into him with the force of a cannon blast.

Slocum felt his chest tightening, heard his own breathing coming harder and harder, felt as if it was too difficult to draw in a breath. He tried to sit up again, tried to thrash out with his arms, but found he could barely move them. His neck tensed and he gritted his teeth, didn't care about the throbbing pain in his head. He thrashed from side to side, howling unintelligible words—he couldn't have survived all that he went through, so where was he? What had really happened?

He eventually became aware of the two voices shouting at him, the weight of their hands holding him down, the woman putting something cool on his forehead.

Then the man said, "I don't care what you say, Julep, I'm a man and I know what a man needs sometimes, and that's a slug of whiskey, by gum, and that's what he's going to get."

Slocum by then had exhausted himself and sagged back against whatever it was he was lying against. He felt the woman's hand on his forehead, heard water dripping, then felt a cloth being put on his head again. "Deke is probably right. He's gone to fetch you a drink. I hope you can keep it down. It'll probably help with the pain. You must be feeling a world of hurt. I only hope I done the right thing in working to save you. For sure you would have died, but you're lucky we all were down here."

"Where . . . where am I?"

"Deke ought not to have said all he did. I shouldn't blame him none, but I will. The big oaf should have kept his pie hole shut tight."

"Where am I?"

"Why, sugar." She smiled down at him, her head canted to one side. "You're down here with us now. In what I call . . . Devil's Canyon."

4

"Oh, hell, Julep, don't scare the man. There ain't nothing that's devilish since we all settled here." Deke came back into view, the light now shining behind his head. "It's Rebel Canyon, if it's anything."

"How's that?" said Slocum, fighting hard to keep from screaming, and to maintain some grip, however slight, on the bizarre situation he found himself in. What if he really was dead and gone and this was some strange other place?

"Don't pay attention to Deke. He's just jealous, is all, because I've spent so much time tending to you when I should have been getting the gear ready—"

"Hush now, girl." Deke's voice took on a darker tone and Julep stopped talking abruptly.

She looked to Slocum as if she'd been caught doing something illegal. But at the moment, he didn't much care, except that all this banter began to feel less like something otherworldly and decidedly more in line with everyday living. That, and he felt like a big old batch of homemade sin, all beat and battered and bruised and throbbing.

"Now," said Deke, leaning close. "You want a drink, boy?

31

It's sour mash, not my best, but it will put hair on the pads of your feet and drop a woodpecker at fifty yards."

Slocum tried to smile, managed something he hoped sounded like a yes. "Help me to sit up."

"Right on it." Deke eased a big arm behind Slocum's shoulders and suddenly Julep appeared, wringing her hands and making sure Deke didn't undo the barely healed results of all her hard tending. Slocum vowed to thank her properly somehow, someday, if he lived. The way he felt at that moment, he didn't dare hope for anything beyond the next ten minutes.

Deke was right—Slocum's nose could tell before the juice touched his lips that it was going to be a potent ride. But he figured if he could keep it down, he'd need it. And deserved it, after all he'd been through. The whiskey lit a bonfire in his mouth, found what must have been a cut and what felt like a busted tooth in the back. He'd worry about that later. Right now, that mash was working its magic. The familiar warmth spread, spilling liquid fire down his throat, gullet, and into his guts before trailing outward toward his fingertips.

"Aahhh," he said, closing his eyes and savoring the relaxing feeling.

"Now there's a man who knows how to enjoy a select mash." Deke's voice reflected the pride of someone whose hard labors have been appreciated.

"Thanks, Deke," said Slocum. "Good stuff, sir."

"Well, I . . . I appreciate that . . . sir."

"Okay, okay, you two. All this 'sir' business ain't going to get biscuits made nor the stew pot boiling, now is it?" Julep's voice receded and Slocum realized he could smell something cooking.

"Chicken?" he said.

"Yep," said Deke. "By gum, but Julep can cook. We're lucky that way. Few of the others are a hand at domestic chores."

"Others?" But if Deke heard him, he didn't let on, just swigged from his bottle.

"Where am I, Deke?"

The big man looked down at Slocum again. "Oh, this here? This is mine and Julep's cave." He must have seen alarm on Slocum's face, because he grinned. "It ain't so bad as it sounds. We got it fixed up nice and pretty. Whole canyon sides are dotted with them."

"What is . . . you live down in the canyon?" Slocum was thinking of the incredible view he had seen of this canyon from above the day before. He assumed it had been the day before. Now he was curious. "How long have I been here?"

"Too damn long, you ask me." The voice was from a different man than Deke. Slocum heard a scuffing sound, then an older man appeared.

"Henry, why can't you be nice?" Julep pushed past the newcomer and fetched something from the shadows, then bustled back toward the mouth of the cave.

"Nice ain't never got nobody nowhere. Ain't that right, Deke?" Henry looked at the big man still hunkered down beside Slocum.

Slocum knew he'd live through this mess, though in what final shape he didn't yet know, as he couldn't get a clear picture of what state his body was in. He recognized that the old man was just a blowhard, probably well-meaning. Slocum thought he'd seen the makings of a smirk on his sunken, toothless mouth.

"So other than too long, how long have I been here?"

Deke cleared his throat and said, "Going on—"

"Hush now, Deke." Julep stood over them, her hands on her hips.

"Why? Man's got a right to know such things."

"It's okay, Julep. I can take it." Slocum tried a smile again and thought maybe he pulled it off, because she sighed, nodded, and threw her hands up. "I have too much to do to stand here jawin' with you all anyway."

Henry appeared to be enjoying this exchange, as his shoulders hiccupped in soundless mirth.

Deke leaned close again and said, "She's just sore because you're not her charge no more. We got a rule of sorts here, when a man goes lame, he's to be tended to only as such time as he can shift for himself."

"And you think I can do that?" Slocum had to ask it, as he felt he could barely lift his own damn head off the blanket.

"Well," said Deke, scratching his bearded chin, "could be I was hasty in that judgment where you're concerned. But I got to keep on top of such things, being mayor and all."

A moment of silence passed. They heard what sounded like the lid of a Dutch oven clank into place, then Slocum said, "So, Deke, you didn't exactly answer my question."

"Oh, that! Well, you been here, um . . ." He drummed two fingertips against his bottom lip. "Pretty near two weeks."

"Two weeks?" Slocum nearly sat up at that startling revelation.

"More like three," said Henry, shaking his head as if he were looking down at a low-life wastrel. "And not a lick of work out of ya."

Slocum let the news sink in, wondered about a hundred different things—the promise of a roundup job he'd been headed for in Nevada. His horse, the trusty Appaloosa, the Apache, the Apache woman, his gear, all of it. "I reckon I'm just lucky to be alive."

Deke nodded his head solemnly. "Yep, you're lucky we done found you, all right."

"Lucky you had Julep to tend to you, is all." Henry flicked open a pocket knife and carved a hunk of tobacco from a black knob of it, then stuffed the thumb-sized nub into his mouth. Slocum wondered how many teeth the old-timer still had.

Deke offered him another swig, and he took it gratefully.

Then Henry spoke. "It was a godawful yelping we heard up there that night." The man looked toward the mouth of the cave, then loosed a stream of thick, brown liquid into the shadows beside him. It showered on what looked to

Slocum like a flat rock, and spattered outward. Judging from his wide smile and filled nostrils, this display of spitting prowess seemed to give the man great satisfaction. "I expect it was you." He nodded at Slocum.

"I expect so," said Slocum.

"Well, it prevented me from getting any more sleep that night."

"My deepest sympathies."

Henry looked down at Slocum, uncertainty twitching one eyelid. "Just see it don't happen again then."

"You have my word, I will do everything in my power to not get attacked by lions, rattlesnakes, and Apache all in one night."

The reaction his comment brought couldn't have been more surprising. Big Deke jumped to his feet, sloshing his precious whiskey. "Apaches? You say you tangled with Apaches?"

I did a whole lot more than that with various Apache, thought Slocum. But to the man he merely said, "Yeah, they're why I'm here. We had a . . . misunderstanding, of sorts." He looked at Deke. "Why? Have you had trouble with them, too?"

It was old Henry's turn to react—he snorted a petulant laugh.

"What's so funny?" said Slocum.

"Trouble, young man, is a mild way of putting it. We been battling those bastards since—"

"Henry!" Deke pulled a deep breath, his massive chest swelling. "That's about enough for now. I expect our guest could use some sleep."

The old man scowled more than he had before, his sunken mouth pulled inward as if he were about to swallow his own head. Touched a nerve, I guess, thought Slocum.

The two men headed toward the cave's mouth. Food smells wafted in and Slocum's gut growled. He breathed deep and closed his eyes, savoring the small bit of pleasure. Then he heard Deke's voice.

"What's your name anyway?"

Slocum opened his eyes. His instinct told him to offer up a fake name. He was a fugitive, after all. But what more could possibly happen to him? It was obvious these people, whatever else they seemed, were certainly not the law. Hell, even if they were, he was so busted up and beaten down that it wouldn't much matter if they were. "I'm Slocum. John Slocum."

Deke looked at him a moment. He nodded, as if agreeing to some voice in his head, and said, "Well, good to meet you, Slocum. I expect we'll be talking more as you heal up. We got need of another man, as it happens. Lots of plans and little time to do 'em in."

The men shuffled on out of the cave and Slocum sank back into the blankets and let his eyes close once again. What in the hell was going on? He'd rarely been in such an odd situation in all his days.

He supposed he should be grateful that he was still alive, after all he'd gone through. And yet he had a strange sense of foreboding that something . . . not quite right was lurking on the horizon. Or more to the point, on the rim of the canyon.

With that thought in his mind, with the warm feeling of sour mash heating his gut, and with the sweet, succulent smells of a chicken-and-biscuit dinner drifting into his nose, Slocum sank into a deep, steady sleep.

5

The next couple of days following his coming around were
curious ones to Slocum. Try as he might, he couldn't get
any further information out of Julep about who the canyon
dwellers were. She just smiled and checked his bandages.
All he managed to do was engage her in mild chatter about
the weather.

It wasn't until he tried to get up and do for himself—
particularly when he felt the need to relieve himself—that
he discovered a way to sort of hold her hostage, and get her
to talk with him in a way that was more honest. She had
been so doting that when he tried to do for himself what
he'd spent his entire life doing, he suddenly realized he was
unable to move his snakebit arm, barely rise up on a wobbly
knee. As the days slowly progressed, he could walk from
one end of the cozy but rapidly confining cave to the other,
yet she seemed more worried about him than ever. He began
to get the distinct feeling she was lonely.

He had been awake in the canyon camp the better part
of a week, which made it nearly a month since he'd tumbled
down there. If Deke, Julep, and their mysterious clan hadn't

37

been down there, he wondered what would have become of him.

One morning, the urge to get up and explore gripped Slocum like nothing had in days. He was grateful for the feeling, for it meant that he was on the mend. He knew from past experience that when he got itchy feet, there would be no stopping him. And to make matters doubly good, he didn't hear the near-constant sound of Julep doing something somewhere close. Most often she was just outside, tending the fire and cooking up meals that had done as much, Slocum knew, to restore his slowly gaining vigor as anything else had. Hell, all of her ministrations were just grand and perfectly revitalizing.

But now, he held his breath before he groaned his way onto his knees, his snakebit arm less than helpful, still throbbing, blackened, but with touches of green and purple, and even a bit of yellowing rising out of the blackness. The poison was leaving his system.

He paused, making sure that she wasn't out there, and when he was satisfied that she didn't seem to be around, he grunted and slowly got to his feet. Cold bullets of sweat stippled his forehead, and a sudden wave of pain lanced with near-nausea rolled over him. He closed his eyes tight and gripped the smooth rock wall with one hand. He forced himself to think of anything but the pain. The wall, the cave, that was it. How long must this place have been occupied? Surely the white newcomers who'd saved his skin hadn't carved these living spaces and occupied the place. Must have been some forgotten vale of refuge for a long-ago tribe.

He'd heard from an old-timer rock hound years before— what was that man's name? Wilkes? Wilkinson? Didn't much matter now, the old man was surely dead—that the West was filled to brimming with all manner of ruins and relics and secret places where ancient peoples once dwelled.

They were people older than the tribes Slocum had come to know, older, he suspected, than most anyone who'd ever set foot in North America. Where had all those ancient people gone to? Slocum had asked the old man, but the duffer had just shrugged his shoulders and gurgled back another long pull of 'shine.

"That's a question for the ages, Slocum," he'd said, before shuffling off westward, ever westward, his burro following along, plenty of slack in the lead line.

Slocum recalled coming across the old man passed out drunk in a heap at the edge of a clearing, one side of his face, neck, and arm badly sunburned, his burro standing patiently by, flicking a long ear occasionally at the sun or an errant shit fly. The beast stood waiting for the old man to rouse himself so they might be on their way to wherever it was those two traveling partners were headed. He knew then that they never really got anywhere in particular, just kept on roving.

And before he knew it, Slocum felt fine again—as fine as he had felt in recent days anyway. He opened his eyes, saw the familiar darkened gloom of the cave, knew that the spell of washing pain had passed, and then, using the wall as support, he made his way toward the mouth of the cave. It was the first time he'd been out there, and he did so under his own steam. And that made him feel pretty good.

He surveyed the scene, saw much more of the camp than he could see from lying on his back at the rear of the cave. It was much bigger than he imagined. The fire ring was a more elaborate affair that someone had taken the time to grout together. And built next to it, an adobe-style baking oven—the reason Julep's bread and biscuits were so darned tasty.

There was also a fine collection of utensils, pots, and pans, and beside that stood a neat stack of firewood flanked by smaller lengths and diameters of kindling. Arranged around the fire were logs for sitting, and a few chairs they must have hauled with them from their Southern homes. All in all, the spot was as tidy as anyone could make it.

Slocum wondered how many folks lived in the canyon. Julep and Deke had been tight-lipped about it. He figured they had their reasons, not the least of which would be because they were doing something outside the law, something that Deke had alluded to a few times and Julep had not said no about when Slocum cautiously questioned her. Then again, she didn't say much of anything about their lives. In fact, she didn't say much at all, just looked at him with that bewitching glance and made him wonder if he was truly in Devil's Canyon, as she'd said . . . She-Devil's Canyon maybe.

Across from the fire, he saw another cave entrance. He closed his eyes once again and breathed deeply. The scent of the junipers and mesquite were intoxicating, and the fresh air and sunlight on his face made him feel better than he had in a hell of a long time.

"What are you doing out here, John Slocum?"

He snapped his eyes open and found Julep watching him, her arms loaded with firewood. So that was who kept the piles topped up. What in the hell did Deke do all day anyway? You'd think that a man would put in a little effort to keep his wife supplied with firewood, at least. Maybe he spent all his time hunting.

Slocum tried a smile on her. "I'm just taking the air, as the dandies say back East."

She slammed the wood on the top of the pile, scattering pieces. "You'd better take the air back in there, mister. Or you'll be sorry."

"Oh, come on now, Julep. I'm not a child and I don't appreciate being talked to nor treated like one, do you hear me?"

That seemed to take some of the starch from her, and she blushed. Yet another change her face underwent that was absolutely bewitching. He'd have to stop looking at her altogether if he wanted to get out of this canyon in one piece, and without Deke's big paw prints around his neck. He was in no shape to fight any man, let alone one built like a granite boulder.

"I . . . I didn't mean to treat you like a child, John. It's just that, you've been so unwell. I . . . I didn't want anything else to happen to you . . ."

She had moved closer to him, stared into his eyes from but a couple of feet away. She was something else, and he had to bite the inside of his cheek to keep from falling again, tumbling farther than he had those weeks before, this time into that woman's stunning gaze.

Slocum cleared his throat. "Look, Julep. I . . . I appreciate all you've done for me. More, much more than you know. I'm so grateful that you happened to be here—or that I happened to pick your canyon to drop into." He tried another smile. It worked a little—she smiled back.

"But you have to realize, I'm a full-grown man—"

"I know that much, John." She stepped closer and he stepped back slowly, leaning against the wall for support. Before he knew it, he was backing into the cave, trying to remain at arm's length from her.

She kept backing him up right to the edge of the cot he'd lain in. "You should lie down, John. You'll be tired, I'm sure."

And damned if she wasn't right. It was as if someone had tugged on all the threads holding him together. And his innards were about to burst the few remaining stitches and weakened seams and he'd collapse in a pile. He forgot about her odd, advancing manner, forgot that he was going to ask her what about Deke, forgot nearly everything in his haste to lie back on the cot once again.

He did, and closed his eyes, felt Julep's familiar, cool hand on his forehead, heard her soothing voice close by his face, and even that didn't alarm him.

Then he barely felt as if cool breezes were dancing in the hair on his chest, but that was impossible—his shirt was on. He roused himself just enough out of his relaxed stupor to open his eyes and see Julep spreading his buttoned shirt wide. Below, his denims somehow had become unbuttoned, too.

"What are you doing?" He struggled to raise his head, but he was in some sort of exhausted half-asleep, half-awake state where nothing made sense.

"Hush now, John. You've gone and tuckered yourself out. You need to rest, relax, and let ol' Julep work her magic."

Slocum couldn't agree more, but he also knew there was something vaguely wrong about all this, but he'd be jiggered if he knew what it was. Just knew he was tired, so damn tired.

The soft breezes stopped, then just before he could force his eyelids to flutter open once again, Julep spoke, this time close by his face, and in a whisper. He felt her warm breath, smelled its coffee-and-honey scent, and heard her voice purr. "You need some of this muscle-relaxing salve I've made, John. It will do you good."

The last thing he knew he needed was anything that might make him more relaxed. Especially when he was pretty sure he knew what was happening—and he was nearly powerless to prevent it. And then two things happened at once: Julep's powerful hands began touching him all over, and a heavenly scent of wildflowers, of honey, of wood smoke, and cinnamon all mingled and filled his senses.

That must be the salve she spoke of, he thought. Wherever those pushing, pulling, kneading hands trailed on his chest, his belly, his arms, his legs, and even below his navel, his skin, his very flesh, tingled and throbbed, but in a comfortable, welcome way. Soon he felt fresh air all over his legs, and he knew she'd peeled off his denims, leaving him nearly buck naked. One last thing remained, the thin undershorts someone—he assumed it had been Julep—had dressed him in way back.

And then he knew that even those had been removed, slipped clean off him while he was busy tingling and relaxing all over. Not a bad life for a man who had assumed he'd fallen to his death. And then those hands began massaging his now fully alert shaft, and even in his advanced state of relaxation, Slocum's breath stuttered in his throat, and worry and pleasure warred for dominance in his mind. "What about Deke?"

Her hands stopped immediately and she paused in her ministrations. She must have looked around her, then sighed and said, "Don't do that to me, Slocum. Now what about Deke?"

"Well, this isn't right. He'll no doubt take us both to task for this."

"Deke? Why should he care? Now stop worrying and let me finish what I started."

Slocum knew that there was nothing he could do or say to change her mind. She was bound and determined to give him a full-body massage. And then he realized she was using more than just her hands. He forced his eyes open and could just see Julep thrusting down her own underpants, hoisting the skirts of her dress high, and gingerly straddling him. In one clean motion, she'd swung a leg over, then slid right down on him, impaling herself and gasping lightly even as she continued rubbing the salve into his chest.

"I've been meaning to give you the full treatment for some time now. But everybody's been here, getting everything ready for . . . just being busy."

Her speech was still a whisper, but came in soft sounds, almost like whimpers, as she worked her slender hips back and forth, fore and aft.

"Don't I have a say in the matter?" said Slocum dreamily.

"Oh, yes, you do. But I happen to know that as your caregiver, anything I feel the need to do to you, such as this"— she stood slightly and reached behind herself and tickled him, making him stiffen even more—"will be far more important and good for you than anything you feel would be good for you, for your best interests."

Her logic bewildered him, but Slocum nodded and grinned through his sense-intoxicated haze. "Whatever you say, Doc."

Julep continued to knead his chest muscles with one aggressive hand while she tickled and stroked him with the other, jerking herself up and down faster with each stiffening reaction he had. Soon, she rose up, nearly off him, but not quite, gripping a handful of his flesh and holding tight. Then, as if she made some reluctant decision, she plunged straight down, once more impaling herself fully on him. They both froze, Slocum gritting his teeth as he pumped and bucked within her, Julep holding her breath, only emitting a tiny cry that dissolved into a sigh.

She soon resumed massaging him with both hands, liberally applying the salve and murmuring about tending to his needs. She never once made an effort to rise up and off him, and neither of them seemed to mind. In fact, Slocum found that he had not diminished in his fortitude in the least. His thickness still filled her and she seemed perfectly content to keep it that way. His worries about Deke were still in his mind, however, and soon he heard himself saying, "What about . . ."

"Deke?" This time she beat him to the finish line.

"Yeah, he's a big fella. Too big, in my weakened state, not to mention our present situation, to pick a fight with."

"Don't worry so much. You think I'd doctor you with so much attention if he was around?"

"What's he up to?"

"Oh, they're gone off to . . . Oh no, you don't."

Slocum swore he heard a smile in her voice. Opening his eyes, however, was not a possibility. She was gently massaging his face now, mostly with her thumbs, and smoothing him from the nose outward and upward. And it felt fantastic.

Soon, he began working her waist around in little circles, matching the technique she was now using on his chest and upper arms. And they were off to the races again. This time Slocum felt like he could contribute a bit more to the process. And it all worked out just fine. At least that's what he remembered as he lay there, sleep slowly overtaking his confused body and mind.

6

A few days later—Slocum tried his best to figure out just how many had passed, but his strength, though gaining each day, was building back up from that of a mewling kitten— and with no warning, Deke strode up to the camp. Slocum was sitting on a chair outside the cave's entrance, recovering from the latest round of working over that Julep had given him. He was getting savvy to her techniques, though, and knew that she'd strike when he was most vulnerable, just after he'd put in a bit of exercise.

She'd not allowed him any weapons, said they would only hurt him, though how, she didn't elaborate on. She also couldn't tell him if they'd found any of his own weapons, save for his boot knife, which she had, only with great reluctance, given back to him. A show of good faith on her part, after he told her in no uncertain terms that he did not appreciate being held prisoner.

She'd protested, said that wasn't the case at all, but then would avoid the topic of how to leave, where the entrance and exit to the canyon were located, and above all, she rebuffed his repeated attempts to find out where Deke and

46

the others—that much he'd gotten out of her, there were other men with him—had gone.

And then, after a few days, Deke strode on up the southward path that Slocum had been slowly trailing, gaining distance down along it day after day. The two men exchanged wordless glances, sizing each other up and down. Finally, Deke broke the silence with a wide grin accompanied with a quick rip of laughter, and then clapped Slocum on his lesssore shoulder. Slocum hoped Deke wasn't just playing him for a fool and that he knew what Slocum and Julep had been up to. Telling Deke he hadn't much say in the matter wouldn't carry much weight.

He wasn't letting on to Julep just how recovered he really felt, but it was substantially more than he let on to her. He felt that keeping her in the dark as much as possible might prove beneficial somehow, though just how he had no idea.

One by one a number of people—young, old, children, and above all, he noticed mostly men, other than old women—began to show up around the campfire. The afternoon had begun to wane, and Deke and Slocum had exchanged a long, boring line of pleasantries. Slocum had eventually just come out and asked the big man what he had been doing, couching it in an offer of help as soon as he healed up enough.

"We'll see, Slocum. We'll just see. For the time being, I'd like for you to meet a few of the folks we have settled here in the canyon."

"Okay, Deke. And since you insist on being so cagey about what it is you do here, I'll go ahead and tell you something about myself. I'm sure it's close to the same thing you can't bring yourself to tell me about you." Slocum eyed the rows of people, young, old, men and women ringing the blazing, snapping campfire, their faces already expectant as they leaned forward. They want to hear what I have to say, thought Slocum. I'll bet they figure it's going to be something great. Well, I'll give it to them.

But before he could speak, Deke gestured toward him

with his big bear face. "You're a wanted man. I bet that's it, ain't it."

The big man's correct guess shocked Slocum for a moment. All he could do was stare back. Finally his eyebrows rose and he chuckled. "Well, yeah, I guess that's about what I was going to say."

Deke held up a ham of a hand. "We none of us wanna hear just what it is you done, nor why you done it. But it does make sense."

"How's that?" said Slocum.

"You being here and all. If I was a man who believed in such things as fate, I'd say you were destined to drop down here like you done."

"But you're not," said Slocum.

"Not what?"

"A man who believes in that sort of thing."

"No sir." Deke rasped a hand under his nose as if he had the sniffles.

"I do." The voice came from Julep. She stood and scuffed a boot toward the fire, dislodging a couple of rocks.

"What about me? Don't I have a say in the matter?" said Slocum. "And what are you so all-fired cagey about anyway?" Slocum figured he'd come right out with it, and addressed everyone. "I've had about enough of this hemming and hawing. It was fine when I was still under your care, but now that I'm healed up, you won't even help me find my way out of here."

"You don't mind my saying it, but you're still in no fit shape to travel. Just how long you think you can survive up there, Slocum?" said Deke.

"I don't know . . . yet," said Slocum. "But I aim to find out."

"Nah, no you ain't neither." Deke shook his head. "'Cause I ain't about to let you."

"You know, Deke, a whole lot of men have tried to best me over the years, but it hasn't much happened yet."

Deke fixed Slocum with a hard gaze. Suddenly a scream sounded from far off, down the little green valley. Deke's eyes perked up. "Oh no! It happened again. We got to go— come on!"

Slocum followed Deke along the west edge of the camp's center fire pit, and others hurried by them, a few ambled along after. As he worked to keep up, Slocum relished the work he was putting his sore limbs through. Any muscles he might have had back when this deadly adventure had begun were now slack shadows of themselves. All the more reason for him to really exert himself. His shot leg throbbed, but a quick glance down at his bandages told him the wound hadn't opened. He'd have to thank Julep again for doctoring him so thoroughly.

The path was beaten down trail that wound along the stream's edge, around boulders, through a couple of marshy spots, and finally they rounded a copse of stout pines. Close by the west edge of the canyon wall a cluster of men stood with their backs to them, tight-packed but fidgety. They looked to Slocum as if no matter how many times they experienced whatever it was they were staring at, it still scared them plenty. As he walked closer, he could see they stood less like men than children; some of them held hands to their mouths.

"Let me through, lemme through!" The big man elbowed his way into the midst of the crowd all staring at a downed man. Then Deke, too, drew up short and gasped. "That's Henry! What happened?" Deke looked up the path, then back down again. Then he looked straight up the canyon side to their right.

Deke bent down near the old man, his big hand checking for signs of life, but even before he shook his head slowly from side to side, affirming what he found, Slocum knew the old man was dead. When a man had seen as much death as John Slocum, one could tell if a man was still among the living just by looking.

Henry was dead; that much was plain to see. His head had been bashed by a rock that had come from on high. The old man lay flat to the ground, his head flopped to one side as if he were in mid-snore, his toothless mouth sagged open. Seeing his puckered mouth pooled with glistening blood and chaw juice reminded Slocum for the briefest of seconds of so many of the battlefield wounds he'd seen back in the war.

Old Henry would never slice a hunk of chewing tobacco off his greasy old knob ever again. He'd never wink or tell a bawdy joke or swig liquor from the bottle or rock back on his heels as if he and he alone were the possessor of vast stores of infinite wisdom. And he truly was a wise man—for who wasn't, really, in this life? thought Slocum. We all are as wise as we say we are, living up to our potentials as much or as little as we dare to in our day's, week's, month's, year's, and lifetime's worth of living.

What happened to Henry was something Slocum very much wanted to hear explained. It looked to him as if Deke had assumed it had been something from above that struck the old man.

"You see that?" said Deke. "Them savages are up against forces they have no idea about. They will all die by my hand or I ain't a Southern man, born and bred."

"You ain't going to do anything of the sort, and you know it," Julep said, not taking her eyes from Henry's still body.

Slocum hadn't seen her come up behind them.

Deke turned to look at her. "Julep, you shouldn't be here. This ain't nothing for a woman to have to see."

"I've seen worse. Remember Slocum when we found him? Now that was a man who looked about done for."

"Aww, knock off the chatter. My old friend's laying here with his head bashed in and you should show some damn respect."

The crowd fell silent, Slocum with them. The old man, Henry, might have been a pain in the ass, but he was likable, too. And a damn sight smarter than most of the men in the encampment. To end up with your head split open from a fallen rock, after having lived all those years, just didn't seem fair. Here was another act that proved to Slocum that life was anything but fair, and far from kind. It also told the loner that it wasn't any old rock that had mysteriously fallen from the tall canyon walls and miraculously hit the old man on the head.

As if reading his thoughts, Deke said, "The foul Apaches did this."

"How can you be sure?" said Slocum.

"Don't mistake my kindness so far for anything but Southern hospitality. Now that you are about healed up, I expect you to pull your share of the load around here."

"And what, exactly, is the load we're all pulling?"

Deke regarded him a moment, then pushed by him on the trail, grim anger clouding his features. "Follow me, Slocum," he said in a low voice. Louder, over his shoulder, he shouted, "Marsden, Pickle, and Jimbo, you keep a watch up above, see they don't pick off anyone else. Tyson and Mary-Bean, you all help Julep fetch Henry back to camp." He looked at Slocum. "Come on."

7

High above, along the rim of the canyon of their forebears, a young Apache brave peered over the rocky edge. Behind him crouched a bellied older man with lines enough on his face to resemble a piece of dried fruit. His moccasin scuffed on the dirt and the youth backed quickly from the edge and spun to regard him. "Grandfather! How long have you been here?"

"Long enough to know that my grandson has done a bad thing. Very bad, indeed."

The boy cast his glance anywhere but at the man who had just reprimanded him. He wished the old man would just leave him alone to prove himself to his father, and to solve the tribe's worries. All at once. If he could but do that, he would earn his father's respect. None of the other men in the tribe had come up with any ideas to drive the hated whites from the canyon.

The boy stood and straightened, flexing his long, lean body. He knew that he had muscled out well and gained more than a head in height above the other young men of the tribe in the last year.

His grandfather knew the boy was proud of how he looked. The young girls of the tribe all stared at him boldly, then when he turned to see the source of their giggles, they would cover their mouths with cupped hands and run away in packs. Silly young things, but he knew their power—and they would soon know it, too. It was the way of all things. And if the tribe ever was able to regain its canyon home, they would need such youths to populate the beautiful place, to carry forth the traditions of his people.

"Grandson, ours is a tribe unlike other Apache tribes. Ours is a tribe apart, all because long, long ago one of our ancestors found the canyon and claimed that untrodden place, that rich lush land where our people chose to stay, to raise animals and even to raise crops. We no longer followed our prey from place to place, but stayed in one place and sent out smaller bands of warriors to bring back game. All was good for our people. We were able to defend ourselves from warring people who found us, for they were few and far between. But then some sickness came among us. We do not know how or from where, perhaps from whites who one of our warriors came into contact with, long before these whites came about among us."

The youth ground his teeth together hard, knowing his cheek muscles were flexing, betraying his outward calm, but he didn't care. He had heard the same story many times. He above all others knew it, and he above all others in the tribe was trying to do something about it! And yet this old man just kept on talking, telling the same story. It was too much sometimes. Though it pained him to keep quiet, he must bite his tongue.

The old man saw the subdued rage and barely restrained mask of calmness on the boy's face, and he kept himself from smiling as he continued, "The sickness took the lives of many of our people. Then it slowed and eventually stopped. We thought we would be well, then. And new babies were born into the tribe, you are one of them, and your friends, the boys and the girls. But as you know, the whites found us. Who knows how, but they did. And they made their way into our beloved canyon, forcing those of us who weren't killed by them to leave, to escape with barely our lives. They took nearly everything from us. We are too few in number to do much more than shake our fists in anger at them, from a great distance, just like old women, nothing more. We are toothless old women."

The youth could take no more of this foolish talk, and spoke. "How can you stand there and tell me this, Grandfather? Do you really think I was not aware of what has happened to our people? Do you not understand why I was here today?"

The boy's chest heaved, sweat had formed on his top lip, and the old man regarded him with a half smile for a long moment. Finally, he spoke, in the same quiet voice he had used all along. "Grandson, if you continue to shout, you shall have your fight with the whites much sooner than you would care to know. Your loud voice will bring them to us as a spring blossom attracts bees. Is that what you want?"

The youth shook his head, glanced downward toward the edge of the canyon a dozen feet away. "No." He looked up at the old man, his eyes glinting in dark defiance. "Not yet."

The grandfather clapped a hand on the young man's shoulder and together they headed to the rocks. "Good," he said. "For I have a plan. But it is not yet ready." He turned to the young man and wrinkled his eyes in surprise.

The youth stopped and regarded the wizened man before him. "But . . . you said I had done a bad thing."

His grandfather nodded, his eyes half-closed sagely. Then he fixed the boy with a piercing gaze. "Yes, but that is only because you should have told me first. Next time, I would like to be the one to push the rock down on the head of one of the whites. We had also better get back to the horses lest they send out angry riders."

The young man could hardly believe what he was

hearing, and yet the old man, his very own grandfather, who walked ahead of him, had just said all that. All that the young man had longed to hear from the rest of the tribe. And now he and his grandfather would work together to conquer the evil whites and drive them from the canyon. But how?

He ran toward the old man, caught up with him. "What is your plan?"

But the old man merely smiled and kept walking toward the rocks where the horses were hidden.

8

Slocum and Deke walked back along the path they had followed, back toward camp, but halfway there, Deke swung
eastward, crossed the brook along stepping-stones put there
for just that purpose. They kept walking for five minutes or
so, then they departed from this new trail and stepped along,
zigzag fashion, through a light, low forest of piñon and scrub
weed. A lanky gray rabbit bolted out from nearly underfoot
just before Deke stepped on it, but the big man never broke
stride.

Slocum knew the big man was upset about Henry. Upset
enough to have stepped on the rabbit and ended its little life
without slowing his pace. Suddenly Slocum caught a whiff
of wood smoke. But they were far enough from camp that
he shouldn't have smelled it. He looked at Deke, who had
slowed and glanced at him.

"So you smelled it. Good. I thought you were someone
who was in control of his wits and senses. Now I'm more
sure than earlier that you'll be a good addition to our band."

Slocum said nothing, just watched the back of Deke's
head as they strode forward. He was beginning to get an

idea of what he was in for, but the next few minutes would, he guessed, reveal all.

And he was right.

Deke stopped abruptly, raised his hands to his mouth, and shouted at the canyon wall two hundred feet ahead, "Hello the camp!"

There was a pause, then a voice shouted, "Come ahead!"

In a low voice, Deke said, "Follow me, Slocum. But don't get rabbity. These boys don't know you yet."

They broke through a man-height wall of vegetation and before them sat a similar setup as the big camp, fire ring in the middle, a couple of logs pulled up beside it, a neat stack of firewood with smaller pieces stacked beside that. The fire was set up with a steel tripod from which hung a black cast-iron pot suspended by a length of chain, and a coffeepot steamed on a flat rock beside the low fire. And beyond, tucked against the face of the cliff, a cave entrance was shielded from above by a rugged-looking roof, not unlike a porch roof off the front of a ranch house, supported by stout log uprights. Slocum guessed that was to protect the "boys," whoever they might be, from rocks dropped from on high.

Slocum didn't have long to wait—appearing one man from each side, two men armed with rifles strode slowly, in measured, cautious steps, the business ends of the weapons not quite pointed at the ground. It didn't appear that they had a problem with Deke, but on seeing Slocum, they slowed their pace and approached with caution.

"Relax, boys. This here's Slocum."

One of the men, a shaggy-looking blond-haired man Slocum didn't think could have been out of his teenage years too long, shifted a wad of tobacco from one side of his mouth to the other. "That the snake man who fell from the sky?"

Deke sighed and said, "Yeah, Doyle. That's him. Only he ain't no snake man, and like I said before, he damn sure can't fly." Deke looked at Slocum, and almost smiled. He turned his gaze on the other boy, who looked to Slocum to be even younger than the first. "Ducky, ease off on that trigger now. I told you he's with me. You hear?"

Slocum had nothing in the way of weapons but his boot knife, which Julep had kindly returned. The rest of his gear hadn't yet been turned over to him, though he'd been told they found a Colt Navy, a skinning knife, and a badly broken Winchester with dented, splintered stocks. That damage had to have been from not just the drop, but from the she-lion's vicious bites.

The young man had to work hard to pry his eyes off scrutinizing Slocum. Finally he looked at Deke and nodded.

"Any coffee on?" said Deke.

"Yeah, we got us near a full pot. You know how Ducky likes hisself a cup now and again."

"Okay, Doyle. What say you go fetch us two more cups. We'll all set here a minute and have us some. I got news for you both."

The two young men both retreated, and Deke watched them head to the cave entrance. He spoke, still watching them. "Unbelievable. Did I tell them both to go for extra cups?" He looked at Slocum, who had followed Deke's lead and sat on a stump of wood.

"You may have noticed, but ain't neither of 'em is right, if you know what I mean. 'Slow' ain't the word. And they can't do a thing apart. I expect they take a piss at the same time, too. But they can shoot the sack off a skeeter at a hundred yards, I tell you what." He nodded solemnly.

"That how come you have them guarding whatever it is you have in that cave over there?"

Deke sat up straight. "How come you to know that?"

"Easy, Deke. I don't know any more than you want me to. I just guessed you had something of value in there. And you just confirmed it. That's it, that's all."

"Well, hellfire. Like I said, you are one of the very sort I need." He was smiling.

"You mind telling me just what it is I'm expected to do for you?"

"All in good time, Slocum. Right now, I got to tell my sons their uncle's dead."

"Sons? And uncle?"

"Yeah, Henry was my older brother. Different mama, but same pap. And yeah, them two award winners are my sons. Bless their mama, she was a looker, but she was not a gifted woman when it come to daily matters such as thinking deep."

"Then Julep, she's your second wife?" Slocum figured he was far enough from the big man's reach that he could ask a personal question without getting a clout from one of those chunky hands. He watched Deke's face redden, and Slocum pulled his head back as he saw the man's eyes widen.

"You thought Julep was my wife?"

"She's not?"

"God no, she's my sister!" His guffaws were so rambunctious Slocum began to feel embarrassed by the noise.

When Deke had settled down and dragged a hand across his eyes, Slocum said, "Then Henry was her brother, too?"

"Naw. Different pap. She wasn't too fond of ol' Henry, bless him. He tried to woo her. Being long in the tooth never slowed him down, but it didn't do much to impress Julep, I can tell you." Deke leaned toward Slocum and grinned. "Why all the questions about Julep? You settin' your cap on my sister?"

"No, not exactly." It was his turn to redden.

"You could do a whole lot worse. She's had offers, of course. But she's as smart as my Ethel was dim. Won't settle for any old fella from the company." He smiled again. "It'd be just like her to fall for a fella who fell out of the sky and on her, in a manner of speaking."

Slocum did his best to ignore the jibing. "What's this company you mentioned?"

Deke's face grew serious again and he slapped his hands

on his knees and stood up. "I expect those boys got all
excited about the stash, figured they'd stare at it all awhile.
Come on and follow me. What I'm about to show you will,
I hope, go a long way toward explaining everything."

They walked to the cave entrance, and just underneath
the porchlike roof, Deke shouted, "Hey, boys, I'm coming
in with Mr. Slocum. Keep your fingers less than itchy." Then
he led the way in.

The interior of the cave was lit by a flickering torch
mounted in a hole in the wall, looked to Slocum to be a rag
soaked in oil and wrapped on a length of branch wood. The
ceiling was vaulted, chipped out of the stone to a height of
roughly a dozen feet at its apex in the center, and the room
stretched back far into the dark. But it was what was inside
the room that pulled Slocum's breath away.

Enough cases and unboxed stacks of munitions to outfit
an entire regiment in a major war battle. Crates marked
RIFLES; six-guns stacked and shiny; ammunition, boxed and
unboxed, gleamed and reflected the dull firelight. A half-
dozen Gatling guns, mounted on tripods, sat like sleeping
vipers awaiting any excuse to spit poison, their dull-metal
heads gleaming thick and solid, their business snouts stilled
but poised.

"What'd I tell you?" Deke waved a big arm toward the
mass of weaponry, smiling as if he'd just announced the
birth of a new child.

Slocum whistled long and low. "That's some stash there,
Deke." He shook his head slowly and took a step forward,
his hand outstretched as if bidden by some uncontrollable
compulsion.

Immediately the two gun-toting young men, one on each
side of the stacks, stepped from the shadows, their rifles
poised on him.

9

"Easy, boys. I told you, Slocum here is with me. And you, Slocum, ease that hand back away from my goods, you hear?"

Slocum complied, hardly aware that he had been reaching toward the stockpile.

"Boys, you can just put up them rifles and do what I asked you to do in the first place."

The boys both looked at Deke. He sighed, rubbed his eyes, and said, "Find me two more cups. We got to have our coffee and I have something important to tell you both."

"Is it that we're finally going to—"

"Do what I say!" Deke's big voice burst any quiet the arsenal might have offered. It worked, though. The boys scurried off to some deeper recess of the chamber, and clattering sounds soon arose from there.

Deke turned to Slocum. "So I guess it's all becoming pretty dang clear to you by now, huh?"

Without taking his eyes off the stockpile of weapons, Slocum said, "Not much, Deke. All I see is a cave filled with brand-new guns of all shapes and sizes—and the ammo to

61

jam in them to make them useful. What that has to do with me, with what happened to Henry, with why you all are living in this hidden canyon—any of it—I don't have a clue." With an effort, Slocum pulled his gaze from the steely curves of a fetching Gatling gun and fixed an inquisitive look on Deke. "But I do hope you are about to tell me."

"I thought for sure you were a brighter boy than all that."

"Nope, not me," said Slocum, still smiling. "But I am an intrigued boy."

"If that's what I think it means, then that's going to have to be good enough for me, I reckon."

Just then the boys clanked and jostled into view from the back of the cave. "Pap," said Ducky. "It just come to me that there was four cups out there by the fire the entire time, just like there always is. We ain't never had them cups in here. You know that."

"So I recall. Oh well, call it my fault. Let's get back to the fire. I got things to tell you. Slocum, too. Besides, I'm not sure I trust him in here alone just yet."

Deke's words sounded playful enough, but Slocum didn't see any mirth in the man's eyes. Not for the first time did he wish he'd ridden the other way when those Apache started their chase all those weeks back.

They trudged back outside, whatever was in the Dutch oven hanging over the smoldering fire and glowing coals had begun to smell downright amazing, and Slocum hoped that the offer of coffee also included a bowl full of the vittles from the pot. His stomach growled like a bear cub backed into a corner.

Once they were settled, with a cup of coffee each in their hands and a tin bowl and spoon for each filled with a bubbling stew, rich in chunks of rabbit, carrots, and potato, they all tucked in. Between bites, Deke spoke. "Boys, your Uncle Henry is dead."

The youngsters reacted as Slocum would expect on hearing such news put to them so abruptly. Considering their obvious deficiencies, or maybe because of them, he wasn't sure which, they took the hard news well. Their lips quivered, their eyes glistened a bit, but they kept silent, listened to Deke's explanation.

Then Ducky burst into the conversation, set his bowl down, and fixed Slocum with a steel eye. "It were him, wasn't it?"

"What?" said Slocum and Deke simultaneously.

"He's the one, ain't he? He's the new one here sent by the Apaches, like you said. Chased by them rascals into our midst. He's the one what killed Uncle Henry."

"No, no, no, no," said Deke, swinging his big, shaggy head back and forth like a grizzly in a defensive pose. "He come to us because of the Apaches, yeah, but that don't mean he is one of them. So put that notion right out of your mind, Ducky. And you, too, Doyle." Deke thrust a thick, long finger at each of them. His look was menacing enough that even Slocum figured were he in their position, he'd comply, too.

Deke turned to Slocum as if nothing had happened. "Now, about them weapons. Surprised as I am that you aren't much in the way of figuring out such things for your own self, I'll just go ahead and tell you, since I have just about run out of time. The guns come from a number of jobs we pulled over the past few years." He paused, half smiling, and waiting for Slocum to react.

"Jobs?" said Slocum.

"Yep, jobs. You see, the folks you've met here only make up about half of who is part of the family, you see?"

"Go on." Slocum could tell that Deke was really warming to his subject. Despite the fact that his half brother had just been killed, his big face grew animated as he spoke.

"Back after the Yankees' war, all the members of our family—even a few who weren't but close friends, though trusted as if they was blood kin—found our way to each other back in Alabama. We tried to figure out ways any of us could make a decent wage after all that killing and stealing and looting by them damn Yankees. And then them even more damnable Yankee carpetbaggers run roughshod right over all that we held near and dear to us—our homes, our land, our crops, our very possessions. Even some of our womenfolks, why there wasn't nothing sacred to a Yankee. They are a cowardly, vicious bunch that death by slow guttin' with a dull spoon is too damn good for."

"How do the weapons come into play?"

"I'm getting to that, mister! Doyle, fetch me another cup of coffee, that's a good boy. Now, you keep on interruptin' me, Slocum, and I swear I will be inclined to believe you are part Yankee. And by God, even to make that thought pop into my head is near grounds for a beating."

"You may throw a beating on me, Deke, but I will tell you right now, it will be the last one you ever throw on a man, you hear me?"

Even Deke's sons gulped.

The big man slowly let a wide smile spread over his face. "There's hope for you yet, Slocum. But don't push your luck with me. That would be a big ol' mistake. Got me?"

"Yeah, I hear you," said Slocum. "By the way, are you close to telling me what it is you plan on telling me?"

Deke sighed again. "Yep. Closin' in on it. So one day, Henry got wind of a U.S. Army Bluebelly plan to transport its pay to all them eager Yanks keeping busy doing the devil's own work of wrangling Indians and making the lives of honest, hardworking Southern folks just as horrible as they can. So Henry says to me, he says, 'Deke, you know what we ought to do? We ought to get our revenge.' 'How's that?' says I. Then he proceeded to tell me just what he'd been thinking of while the rest of us had been sitting around on our hands, not doing much of anything except complaining."

"So you robbed a Yankee payroll train?"

"Yep, and it went so well we did a few more such jobs. Then we hit a big haul, a weapons train. We didn't really figure we'd ever use that many weapons. But our loot piles had grown so big that we had to find better places of storing it. Plus, we knew it was just a matter of time until the law would track us down. We were made up of family, after all, men, women, children, a few farm animals. That sort of thing. We decided to head west, and once we got rolling, we kept telling each other that we would keep on going until we found a spot we couldn't stand not living in. But funny thing happened on our way to our promised land." Deke smiled at Slocum, his eyes twinkling.

"Let me guess—you got lost out here."

"See now, that's why I think you might just make a decent addition to our little clan, even though you ain't nothin' but a man, though I know you're a Southern man. So that has to count for something. The rest, though, that don't mean much. You want to impress me and the clan, you woo my sister, then we'll make you a full-fledged member. Until then, you just listen to the rest of this story."

Slocum suppressed a smile with a sip of coffee.

"So we got lost, all right, just as you say. But getting lost never worked out so good as it did for us all those years ago. We ended up here, in this pretty place."

"You mean to say you just sort of fell into it?"

Deke laughed, slapped his knee. "Naw, only a fool would do such a thing as that!" Then his face grew somber once again. "We was up above, on the flats, and figured to hunker down for the night, make a fresh start of it in the morning. We got the wagons arranged, the pulling beasts unhooked, and had our evening meal. Could be we'd been a mite too carefree about our safety, our drinking was such that I am sure our voices carried a long way off on the breezes that night. But it was hot and we were tuckered out and we hadn't had much trouble one way or t'other with Indians."

"But that night was to prove your undoing, eh?" Slocum inquired.

"Yep, that's a fact." Deke stood, tossing to the ground the last of the now-cold coffee in his cup. "After all the family had been through in the war, and after it. After all the hard work and deaths and whatnots . . . you'd think there would be somebody somewhere, maybe up in big ol' heaven, who might say, 'Gosh, that don't look right. Them are good people. Must be some mistake.' But no, nobody lent a hand to help us. Them Apaches attacked us when we were asleep, They killed babies, women, it didn't matter to them. My sweet wife had barely got over a creeping sickness, but a . . ."

Slocum heard the man's breathing come harder, hitched and thickened.

"Arrow took her in the eye. Never stood a chance, poor thing. A pile of others, too. We rallied and managed to hold them off as best we could. But they drove off most of our animals. We had a few lone nags left, a couple of milk cows. The next morning dawned hot as the blazes, the flies begun their buzzing and the buzzards their death dances. Then someone who went to track our cattle and fetch water come back presently and told some of us that he'd found the promised land. We knew he wasn't what you call slow, so we half believed him."

"Anyhow, a few of us followed him for a bit, just to humor him, we thought. But we found not only water, but a long, winding entrance to this here valley."

"Seems like you decided to stay," said Slocum.

"Yep, but what we didn't know was something we'd find out before long. The canyon was as pretty as a picture—what we could see of it anyway. But as we explored, we nearly lost our heads in the process. It was filled with Indians— Apache. Seems they got here way before us. But we ain't nothing if not inventive, and soon enough, we had them Apaches—what was left of them—on the run, squawking and hollering and yowling to beat the band. We spent the better part of two weeks fighting them no-goods, but we finally won enough that we got all the way down into the canyon. And we managed to keep most of our livestock, too, which they had conveniently pastured off down here, though they'd been eatin' off it for two weeks, the rascals."

"We chased them Apaches out of here, gave 'em a good whuppin', no doubt about that. This here canyon is a good place for us, to be sure. Lots of fresh water, green plants, places to plant gardens, there's game—even deer—in here, plus we bring in our own supplies."

Deke refilled their cups, then took his seat. Both boys stood and stared at their father as if it were the first time they'd heard the strange tale. But Slocum bet they'd heard it plenty of times before. "What happened to the Apache, then?"

"We run 'em off, thought maybe for good, but a few months after that, they started with the sneak attacks. Can't leave well enough alone, seems to me. We whipped them fair and square, then they go and start stealing from us again, picking us off one at a time."

"Sounds to me they're behaving just like a lot of Southerners have in the South, following the war."

"Now that ain't fair and it ain't right, no, not at all. First off, the North didn't win that war; they stole from us and then hung us out to dry. And then they came back and stole from us. So by my line of thinking, the only one that matters round these parts, by the way, what we're doing—liberating money and arms from Bluebellies—is payback for their criminal ways. And little enough at that. I had my way, all them Yanks would swing from the highest tree."

Slocum figured he'd keep his peace. He wasn't sure how many nerves he could get away with prodding and poking where this man was concerned. But Deke blazed right on ahead with his story.

"So what we done was start an all-out war with them rascals. And in the meantime, I sent a handful of men up and out to pull off a few jobs, and fetch more folks back, recruits, you could call them. As you can see, this here canyon has plenty of goodness in it for lots of folks, more than we have now. But what I really wanted them other folks here for was to help deal with the Apaches. They're a sneaky bunch, laying in wait, then ambushing us."

Slocum couldn't help himself—surely Deke saw the similarities between what he said the Apache did and what he and his band of marauders did. "Sounds a bit like what you and your men do, eh, Deke?"

The big man crossed his arms like a petulant child, but Slocum could see the vein in his forehead throbbing. Hell, he thought. I've barely begun to heal and I prodded too hard on one of the biggest men I've ever met.

Slocum started to get to his feet, hoping to make it a fair fight. But Deke turned, half smiling and shaking his head, and said, "I reckon you're right, ol' Slocum. But I don't feel bad about kicking them Injuns out of this here bountiful canyon. And you know why?"

"Why, Pa?" Doyle's wide eyes regarded the big man with awe. His younger brother, Ducky, looked as stricken.

"Why, boys, because they took your mama from us. And they didn't need to raid us. Hell, if they had left us be, we'd likely have moved on in the morning. But they had to pick a fight. And as my own dear departed pap used to tell me, boys, and now you listen good 'cause I'm about to impart wise words to you, you hear?"

The two young men nodded like fresh recruits given their first orders.

"He used to say, 'Deke-Boy,' that's what he called me, but only he could get away with that. He'd say, 'Deke-Boy, don't you never start a fight, but if someone picks a fight with you, then you by gum be the one to finish it.'" He ended by pointing a big sausage of a finger at his enraptured sons.

"So," said Slocum. "You're just working on finishing the fight the Yankees picked with you and yours way back?"

"Yep. Ain't you been listening?"

"You still haven't answered the big question, though,

Deke," Slocum drained the last of his coffee and set the cup on a rock.

"What's that, Slocum?"

"What you plan on doing with that arsenal you have stockpiled in that cave yonder."

"I was getting to that, by gum. I was gettin' to it!" He ran a big hand through his curly graying hair and rummaged his thick fingertips in his beard as if he might find an answer in there. "It's all about the Apaches, you see."

Slocum nodded. That much he'd gathered from the previous half-hour's worth of chatter. He did his best to suppress a sigh.

"Pap's getting to it, Slocum!" Ducky had sprung to his feet and fingered his rifle lovingly.

"Ease off, youngster," said Slocum to the surprised lad. "I've had enough of you and your hotheaded brother." Slocum cut his eyes to Deke. "Now either get to the point, Deke, or let me leave this canyon of yours. I'll take nothing, but leave my eternal gratitude to you and Julep for saving my life. But I won't be prodded, nor manhandled, nor intimidated by children with guns. And I won't be kept prisoner, not when I've done nothing wrong, nothing to offend you."

Slocum matched the big man's glare second for second, all the while his arm throbbed, as it had from time to time since he'd awakened from the snake bites, the fall, all of it. The skin, especially around the puckered wound, had gone black, but had luckily healed—slowly. And though he still didn't have full use of the hand, he was gaining on it every day. But not enough to swing a punch, especially not at someone like Deke.

Once again, Deke surprised him by telling the boys to sit down. Then he said, "Fair enough, Slocum. Those weapons in there are to use against the Apache, maybe even a few Bluebellies sometime. Some of my people want to move out beyond the canyon, settle on the rim. But the Apaches are a thorn in our paw, have been since we got here. So I've been stockpiling arms until we had enough men and guns to take them out once and for all."

"And now you do?"

Deke smiled. "With you and your obvious skills as a leader, plus your war experience, the fact that you're a Southern man, that my sister's sweet on you—and I think you are a bit on her, too. Plus the fact that as a Southern man—and so, a man of honor—you are feeling not a little beholden to me and mine for saving your skin. Most importantly, the fact that my people seem to think you are some sort of magic man, a bit like an Injun shaman, of all things, well, that just takes the cake."

"Because they'll do what I say then?"

"They'll do what I say, friend. And if I say to do what Slocum tells them . . ."

"And I'm doing what you tell me . . ."

"See? You are a wise one. Can I pick 'em, boys, or can I pick 'em!"

"You can sure pick 'em, Pap," Doyle said. Then he leaned forward and, in a lowered voice, said, "Pap, is he really a magic man?"

Deke let out one of those rolling belly laughs and said, "Son, he just might be, he just might be at that!"

Slocum wanted to tell Deke that all he was hearing was mumbo jumbo, that Deke was setting all this up, saying all those things only because he wanted an excuse to kill the Apache. But he had a feeling that if he did say that, ol' Deke-Boy, no matter how much he said he wanted Slocum working for him, wouldn't tolerate much more in the way of back talk and defiance.

Slocum suspected that on the surface Deke was a kindly, guffawing man large of heart and generous of his time, but as leader of this seemingly well-oiled band of backwoods, deep-South crack shots, outlaws, and ne'er-do-wells, he had to rule with a fist of steel in order to keep law and order— his law and his order.

That would account for why Slocum saw so little discord in the camp—at least what he'd seen of it so far. If what Julep said and what Deke hinted at were true—and he saw no reason to doubt—then the canyon had a half-dozen such camps along its length. If there were up to a dozen people at each camp, women, children, and the older folks included with the fighting-age men, then there might well be seventy-five, eighty, or more members of Deke's big, sprawling rebel family.

And if that were the case, he guessed those numbers would equal or outnumber those of the Apache. But what would really tip the scales were the weapons that Deke's people would use. Those Apache would be cut to ribbons in minutes. And that would be one less Apache tribe in the West, in the world.

Slocum knew, despite his problems with the Apache, that he wished them no ill will, that mass slaughter was something Slocum could not promote nor tolerate.

But how could he possibly foil Deke's plans? First things first, Slocum, he told himself. Find out what Deke had in mind, and most important, when he wanted to do the grisly deed.

As if reading his mind, Deke swallowed another splash of coffee and said, "Now that you're well enough to stand up to me—and I respect a man who will do such a thing—to a point, that is—why, I'd say we are just about ready to assemble to fighters in the family and track those snakes to their foul Injun den." His mouth split into a grit-toothed sneer and his eyes took on a glazed look.

"And once we do, we'll trap them inside and cut to ribbons every last damn one of them. We won't stop with just the braves. Oh, hell no. Because kids grow up and breed and make more murderous Apaches."

Slocum wanted to point out, one last time—though he knew it would be far from the last—that that was exactly what Deke's people were doing. Breeding more angry fighters. It was just like one of those old silly mountain family grudges from way down South, and he expected the same thing happened in the East, the North, and the West.

Didn't matter where, because people were the same the world over. If they could fight, they would. Just to prove that they weren't willing to admit that maybe they didn't know right from wrong, didn't have all the answers. This sort of hatred fueling Deke would never end. Unless someone put a stop to it. Slocum knew that was a thankless job but one that sadly he seemed ideally suited for. He sighed and looked at the big, smiling criminal.

"When do we begin?"

Deke clapped a big ham hand on Slocum's sore shoulder and said, "Ha ha! That's the very dang question I was hoping you'd ask. Proves to me I was right." He turned to his boys and said, "Take care of things here, boys. I'll be back shortly. First, I have to introduce Slocum to a few folks."

"The brothers, Pap?"

"Them's the ones, Doyle!"

As they walked from the camp, Slocum heard the peculiar Ducky and Doyle giggling and hooting like monkeys, and he wondered how it was all going to work out.

10

Any thoughts Slocum had of heading back to the cave for a little rest slipped right out of his frazzled mind when he heard Deke's plans. Now he had no time to waste in forming some sort of plan to head off this nest of crazies from wiping out his own enemies. What sort of a situation have I got myself in anyway? he thought.

Slocum shook his head as he followed Deke on yet another all-but-invisible trail farther down the canyon. This time to meet yet more mysterious brothers. Were they all related? And where in the hell were all the young women? So far he'd seen a whole lot of menfolk, kids—mostly boys, come to think of it, though there were a few girls mixed in—and very few people of the female persuasion, save for Julep and a few older ladies. And the ones he had seen were not the sort a man should be looking at. They were either toothless crones or spindly-legged tomboys.

No wonder poor old Henry wanted to tuck his boots under Julep's bed. Slocum couldn't blame him—the pickings were slim elsewhere in the canyon, and Julep was one hell of a woman. He'd rarely seen her equal. All blond hair and hazel eyes that he knew saw more in him than he was letting on. It was unnerving, in fact, to look up from a task and find her staring at him, one eyebrow arched and the opposite mouth corner curving upward in the beginnings of a devilish grin, as if she'd just discovered something about him, something that excited her.

And he'd found out just what that look meant. She was a wild thing, and had a body to back up that unspoken claim.

Slocum nearly walked into Deke's broad back when the big man slowed his pace. He cursed himself for not paying more attention to where they were going, instead of just following blindly, dumbly, like a kid. His ailments must have taken more out of him than he realized. He was usually more aware, sharper than this.

He looked around, curious to know why Deke had slowed his pace, and saw they were threading their way through a thicket of bushes just before a greensward. But they weren't going to cross the meadow. They were staying well within the tree line, and Deke was eyeing the sun-dappled meadow grass. Slocum instinctively lowered himself into a crouch, his finely honed senses of a fighting man telling him something dangerous was likely crouched not far away in the grass. And that something might well be eyeing them with as much caution—and the decided advantage of sight.

Slocum saw a flash of buckskin, heard a high-pitched snicker, and dropped down even lower in a crouch. By then, Deke had stopped walking forward and glanced sideways at Slocum. Instead of alarm on his face, as Slocum had expected, he saw a smirk.

This man is crazier than I thought. Suddenly not ten feet from Slocum, just to his right, up popped a tall, thin person clad in buckskins. The skins, a patchwork haphazardly lashed together with rawhide scraps, did nothing to hide the fact that this figure belonged to a woman who, though tall, bore curves in all the right places. The rest of her, unfortunately, was a savage-looking affair.

She stared at them, slowly waving the large, flashing blade of a skinning knife back and forth before her face, like the tail of a slowly aroused pit viper.

It didn't take long before this act grew old. Slocum had been in plenty of situations where such hollow displays of posturing had led to the perpetrator backing down, backing away as if he'd accomplished something impressive by merely waving his weapon menacingly or sneering as if he were about to bite off the head of anyone who dared step closer.

"Am I supposed to be impressed?" he said. He couldn't help himself.

Suddenly the raw-looking woman growled and did just what he'd have guessed she'd do—she eyeballed him with what he was sure was supposed to be menace and bone-chilling hate while stepping slowly backward. The only part of the display that was impressive was when she melted back into the trees. Though she was close, he lost sight of her sooner than he'd expected to. So she did know a thing or two about disappearing into her surroundings. He'd keep that in mind. Now if her siblings or cousins or whatever they were shared her talent, he could well be surrounded right now and not know it.

"Just what was that, Deke?"

"That's my cousin, Rufus," said Deke.

"Rufus? But . . ."

"I know what you're thinking, but don't let on, you hear?" whispered Deke. "She's mighty sensitive about that. Thinks she's a man. Been acting like one her whole life, but she's a dang good shot, and in the end, what with the troubles we all been through, we figure that's about all that matters. So we leave her be. Family don't pay her no never mind, and she's private and all, so it don't much matter what she wants to be. Hell, she could take up being a chicken and we'd all just go along with it, I reckon. Long as her shootin' stays as good as it is anyways."

"And I bet you could use the eggs, too." Slocum thought his joke would be appreciated by Deke, but if the man understood what he'd said, he didn't let on.

Deke looked at Slocum with a set jaw and squinted eyes. "It's the blamed strangers who make it tough for the odd ones. Folks like that usually end up causing a fuss, riling everybody, then skedaddling in the night. That's the way it always happened back at Durfee's Holler. I reckon the canyon ain't no different."

"No need to worry about me. Unless it's that I might die of curiosity before we get there."

"Okay, okay, Slocum. But these cousins of mine are what you might call a little jumpy."

"Deke, nothing much would surprise me anymore. If you hadn't noticed, you are talking to a man who should be dead right about now. Remember?"

The big man laughed. "Come on. They won't tolerate being kept waiting." And with that, he led the way forward through yet another dense thicket. Shortly, the thick scrub parted before them to reveal a small grassy sward similar to the one they'd seen a few minutes earlier. Slocum guessed it was another pasture for beasts.

So far, he'd not seen any horses, milk cows, or even chickens. Though he thought one morning he swore he heard a rooster crowing far to the south, the direction the canyon stretched. He couldn't wait to explore its full length soon. Then find his way out of there, warn the Apache of the undefeatable weapons Deke was ready to launch against them. And what they did with the information was up to them, he figured.

His only other option was to blow up the munitions right where they sat. Not a bad idea—destroy them before they got transported out of the canyon. He'd have to give that one some thought.

His biggest problem with that lay in the fact that he had no weapons other than a boot knife. He was also still moving as slow as an old man gripped with ague and rheumatics, as the old-timers called it, and the cave full of weaponry and ammunition was guarded by two dimwitted brothers. Okay, so he could probably handle those boys at first. However, if they really were solid shots, he wasn't so sure he was going to be able to sneak in there and out again without detection.

Time will tell, Slocum said to himself. Keep taking in information, maybe learn something about this batch of crazies I fell into . . . And then they were surrounded.

Just what he hadn't expected to happen did happen—a tall, thin man in buckskins, more leather patch than solid garment, emerged from the foliage almost as though the trees themselves were receding into the background. Off to Slocum's left another materialized out of the woods. He was nearly identical to the first, save for the expression on his face and the length of the patchy beard. They each carried what looked like a Kentucky long rifle. And there was something else odd about them—something about their faces, their eyes, their way of staring at him. Then he knew—they were nearly dead ringers, albeit male versions, of the woman Deke had called Rufus. How many more were there?

One of them squinched up one eye, worked his bunched jaw up and down as if he were considering a difficulty, then sluiced a long, tailing stream of chaw juice. Half of the viperlike stream slapped against his crusty buckskins and glistened in his beard. He dragged the back of one hand across his mouth and snuffed in a quick gasp of air through his nose, as if he were snoring. "You . . ." He pointed at Slocum.

The other one, who also had been busy spitting, said, "Who you?"

Deke held up his hands as though he were keeping them apart. "Now men, just keep your peace a minute, will you? I'm fixing to tell you all about this here fella." And Deke proceeded to explain who Slocum was and how he came to be there.

"Where are the rest? Back yet?" said Deke, by way of finishing the conversation.

The first one to speak snorted again, spit, then said, "Nah, not yet. I reckon they're—"

"Still on one of your jobs," the other one said, finishing the thought. "Be back directly."

"Aw hell, that's too bad."

"Why you here, Deke?"

"Bad news, I'm afraid, boys. Ol' Henry's up and died on us." Deke's face grew tight and he looked at his boots.

"What?" said the first as he pulled his sleeve from his beard.

"How?" said the other.

Deke didn't look up, and Slocum wondered if he was going to tell them the truth. Deke skittered his glance toward Slocum then said, "Apaches."

It was as if he'd thrown a stick of dynamite into a crowded street. Both men began yammering at once, then yelling for Rufus. She emerged from the woods, dead ahead of them, no weapons in her hands. She seemed to be the only one besides Slocum who wasn't yelling at the top of their lungs.

But she was making sounds, weird growling, angry sounds. And she rarely took her eyes off Slocum. But instead of the attention he was used to receiving from women, this one shot daggers of hate at him from her eyes. The spite in those near-black orbs was intense.

He broke off his gaze from hers and rushed forward to help Deke, who had his hands full with the two tall, thin, buckskin-clad men, who both appeared to want to tuck right into him. They crowded him with their bony chests, arms down by their sides, rifles held back. This aggressive posturing was almost comical. It looked as if two skinny roosters were intent on bothering a massive barnyard dog.

Curiously enough, Deke did little more than take it. Was he afraid of them? That notion seemed impossible.

As soon as Slocum grabbed the arm of one—the second

of the two to have spoken earlier—he spun on Slocum and began his crazy pushy chicken dance with him. Slocum pushed right back. And it felt good, despite the fact that the skinny woodchuck directed his tirade at him. Slocum really wanted to punch the man in the face.

Finally, Deke got the crazies calmed down enough so that they weren't pushing, and their yammering had dwindled to argument levels.

"I told you," said one, "we got to get on up there right now."

Deke nodded in agreement, but said, "And I told you when them boys get back, we'll organize and ride on out, with wagons loaded and hell a-blazing. But them idiots still ain't back, so we got no choice but to wait."

"We don't need them!" shouted one of the brothers. "We got us, and you still got a few boys down to your fancy end of the canyon, ain't you?" The man gave Slocum a glance. "I don't suppose you know how to use a gun."

As he said it, he rubbed a grimy hand along the stock of his rifle. As filthy as he and his brother were, their weapons gleamed, spotless, ding-free, and well oiled.

"I've been handy with one a time or two, yeah." Slocum suppressed a smirk and turned to Deke.

Deke pulled himself up to his full height and bellowed at them. "Slocum here ain't going to fire up his gun, ain't going to do nothing without my say-so and whenever I say so, you got that?"

The effect was impressive. They backed down like scalded pups and looked at their feet. "Aw, Deke, they kilt Henry! We got all them guns and . . . and . . ." the skinny man blustered, his head shaking in bewilderment. "Well, dang it, Deke, Henry's dead!"

The other one picked up. "How many more of us all they got to kill afore you cut loose with them guns?"

"Yeah, yeah, dang it!"

The entire time the two men ranted, working themselves up into a new lather, their sister, Rufus, stood off to the side, not once taking her eyes from Slocum, but pantomiming their rising rage with arm thrusts and leg kicks, and emitting howls that sounded more like animal utterances than those from a young woman.

What a family, thought Slocum. How do they ever get anything done? How on earth did this man and all these crazies ever manage to steal all that military plunder?

Once more, it looked as if Deke were gathering a lungful of air to bellow his big bear voice at the men. But something else happened before he could shut them up once again.

The two buckskin-clad men backed away from him. One of them shouted, "We'll do it ourselves, then." And before Slocum could reach out and grab the nearest of them, the men ran northward, toward the direction from which he and Deke had just come, toward the cave filled with weapons watched over by Deke's slow-witted sons.

The men were fast, faster than Slocum had seen anyone move in a long, long time. Except for that time he'd had to pile on out of that second-story ranch house bedroom window because the man of the house had returned from a trip unexpectedly. And Slocum had been in a state of near-complete undress, save for his hat and boots, and in bed with the woman of the house.

Not one of his finest moments, as he recalled. He'd lost wages, a good shirt hung up on that cottonwood tree close by the porch, and he hadn't even got to finish what he'd started. Still, the memory almost made him smile as he followed Deke back toward the cave.

"Rafe! Ralph! Come back here!" the big man shouted, obviously distressed. Slocum imagined that his thoughts were with his boys, hoping like hell the two buckskinners weren't capable of what Slocum guessed they really were— killing the boys if it meant getting to those weapons.

"Would they harm your sons?"

"Naw, I don't believe it. But I can't let them get at them

guns. Not yet. We got to organize this mess. That's how we will beat the Bluebellies, in the end . . ."

For a brief moment, as they loped through the brush nearly side by side, Slocum caught Deke's eyes, wide and set in a tense face.

So that's it, thought Slocum. His real aim in all this is to take on the entire United States Army. And the Apache are just a convenient bit of warming up, a practice attack, so to speak. No wonder he's protective of the weapons he has. He'll need a whole lot more if he's going to take on the army. And speaking of, where's he going to get an army to fight an army? He hadn't seen but a few dozen fight-worthy folks in all the valley.

Slocum figured he'd better make light of it, as if Deke's slip of the tongue didn't matter to him. "Anybody behind us?" shouted Slocum.

"No! They're the last ones before the end."

Slocum could tell Deke had been about to say more, but even in that heated moment he kept his mouth shut and ran.

"Slocum, you head off that-a-way, and try to keep Rufus from rousting my other men over to where Henry died! They're tense and angry and liable to break. Wouldn't take much! I have to get to the cave and see to it that my boys hold strong!"

Slocum nodded and headed where Deke indicated, looking for all the world as if he were in lockstep with the man. And nothing could be further from the truth, he thought. As soon as Deke crashed off through the undergrowth and out of sight, Slocum slowed, then stopped, catching his breath. He'd wait a few seconds, make sure he heard no one heading back toward him, then he'd head for the southern end of the canyon.

It was time to pursue his freedom, sooner than he imagined he would, but another opportunity like this might not come along, at least not before Deke mustered his troops and readied for the attack on the Apache. Unless the crazy buckskin brothers got their way and overpowered Deke and his boys. The thought gave Slocum slight pause. Deke might be a bit on the crazy side himself, but he and Julep had treated him well enough. It was what Deke had planned for him, though, that once again set Slocum's feet to heading with all resoluteness toward the southern end of the canyon.

And that was when he smelled it—the foul, damp reek of piggish human sweat. And not his own—he'd never in all his days smelled that off. No, this was the aroma of someone long used to going without a washing, and someone whose diet probably consisted of rancid meat and runny dung. He didn't dare move any more than he had to, despite the fact that the stench had begun to water his eyes. He slithered his hand downward to his boot, felt the reassuring haft of the boot knife. It was all he had, but he'd often made do with a whole lot less.

Whoever had crept nearby didn't seem to know he was there, a foot or two from them in the bushes. He hoped like hell it wasn't one of those feral kids, but if it came down to it, he'd do his darnedest to fend off the stinking creeper. Whoever it was shifted weight, stepped on a stick, snapping it and eliciting a grunt. Slocum shifted only his eyes, squinted through the dense pack of spindly branches, and saw a snatch of buckskin. Could be Rufus, Rafe, or Ralph. It didn't much matter to him. Then the stranger spoke, in a singsong whisper, but meant for hearing.

"Come out, come out, you dang rascal. I got me a long-ass toothpick and I intend to gut you, you flyin' snake man."

Yep, meant for him. Still couldn't be sure which of the three it was, but he knew they all carried big Arkansas toothpicks swinging from their waists. And side arms, and long guns, and teeth and claws. What he had to do was outwit this stinking hick. And a thought occurred to him. He knew just what he needed to do, or at least the only thing he figured he could do. He'd find out in mere seconds if this was a good idea or not. If not, he wouldn't have too long to wait.

He slowly lowered himself even closer to the ground, the pain in his wounded leg lancing up his side, forcing him to grit his teeth. If he bit together any tighter, he'd powder them. He waited another second, knife gripped tight, then he hissed, *"Pssst!"*

The reaction was so fingersnap quick, it was as if a rattler were spooked from behind or a snoozing wolverine were prodded with a stick. The brush exploded in a growling brown blur, stink flowing with it as the rogue rebel launched at Slocum. He dropped to his shoulder, rolled with it as the attacker landed on top of him. Raw meat stink clouded Slocum's nostrils, filled his mouth, nose, and lungs. He grunted in part from the sudden weight atop him, in part from the pain in his wounded leg, his snakebit arm, his whole-body bruising, and his still-throbbing skull.

Slocum felt the attacker, but he still couldn't tell if it was Rufus or her brothers, all bone and muscle, stretched sinew, lean and snarling. It was as if he were fighting the she-lion all over again, so powerful was this writhing demon. He caught sight of slashing, brown-tinged teeth, a couple of them decayed blackened stubs, almost pointed as if fangs. The face lunged at him and he could tell now by the lack of whiskers on the begrimed cheeks that it was Rufus.

She raised a long, thin blade high above her head, and slashed it downward at his face. Slocum grabbed the bony wrist with his snakebit hand, but it was a losing battle. His arm was still weak. The great strength that he had spent his adult life working on and building up was just not there yet, was not built back up to the level he needed it to be.

But that didn't stop him from redoubling his efforts, and with a quick, clipped bark of pain and rage, he jammed upward with both hands, the knife angled away from the attacker so he didn't kill her just yet. At the same time he managed to raise one knee and ram it into Rufus's gut.

The effect was immediate and just what he'd hoped to do—the freakish tomboy woofed, air gouted from her mouth, and her dark eyes widened and bulged.

He'd knocked the wind from her, and after a few seconds she groaned and began moaning as he quickly rolled to the side, keeping the she-devil at arm's length. He continued the roll, ended up on top of her, and managed to pin her wrists to the spongy earth of the patch of thicket, one of her grimy claws still clutching the big skinning knife, one grasping like the fast-flexing talon of a raptor.

Slocum still clung to his boot knife, and where it nested between his quivering palm and her grasping hand, he pressed it hard. They stared into each other's eyes; every part of her face but those dark angry eyes kept up a constant twitching movement of anger. But those eyes, oh those eyes, they bore into his, never once wavered, and in them he saw hate and rage and confusion and anguish and spite, boiling in the brown-black depths. This was one creature who would never know love, he thought. And this is one creature I have no interest in trying to explore those possibilities with.

During this intense struggle, neither of them emitted much more noise than the occasional grunt, hard-expelled breath, or hushed gasp. If he didn't know better, it could have been a fresh round of sex they were participating in. Even her bucking, thumping, writhing rhythms mimicked the power many a woman had elicited under his ministrations.

But this was one situation that was entirely different. He had no idea what was going to happen next, but since he was in charge, at least for the moment, he knew he had to make the next move—and quick.

But he didn't make that next move quick enough—she did. One second, Slocum was staring down at her hate-filled eyes, formulating a quick plan to render the irate woman immobile, the next he was seeing stars. She'd rammed her head upward hard and popped him one on the forehead with hers. It wasn't a hard enough hit to force him off her fully, but it was enough to loosen one of his clamped hands from hers. She wasted no time in lashing his face with the freed claw.

It stung and he felt his cheek bleeding, but he counted himself lucky—it could have been his eye. And still might if he couldn't get this devil under control again. His free hand held his boot knife, and in her thrashing haste to free herself, Rufus slid her hand across the fixed blade. She howled and pulled the hand back, her instinctive reaction. But it didn't last long. She was waving the foul thing at him again, spraying blood and making increasingly louder noises of anguish now.

That would bring her brothers and who knows how many others they had stashed in the woodwork around the camp, all scampering to help her. Up until she'd slashed his cheek with her dirty paw, Slocum hadn't wanted to hurt her. But now he didn't care. He figured it wasn't man and woman fighting any longer, but two enemies, one bent on killing the other. And he had no intention of being killed. So he rammed his left knee hard into her gut.

And the effect, since he had the advantage of dropping, driving weight, did what he hoped—it stopped her cold. She made a slight mewling, gagging sound. He snatched the big skinning knife from her opened hand and wedged it in his belt, then stuffed his own knife back in his boot.

While she was still incapacitated, he peeled off her own belt, a raggedy hair-on affair, and flipped her over. Just before he did, he saw not anger in her eyes, but fear, the first time he'd seen that on her face in the last few minutes of struggle. He guessed that she wasn't used to feeling anything akin to fear. What was she thinking he might do to her?

He forced both her wrists behind her and lashed them together, snugging the hairy belt as tight as he could. It wouldn't hold her for long, since there was no buckle, just floppy leather sporting patchy brown-black hairs, like the beard on a teenage boy. But it would have to do. She'd also worn a coil of greasy rope that dangled from a thong on her belt. He didn't tie her up with that because if his plans worked out, he might need that rope. He transferred the coil to his own belt and stood up cautiously, looking around for anyone else who might be lurking nearby, but saw no one.

Before he left her there, he bent low, but not close enough to her head to take another whack from that thick skull. "You really should try to be nicer to people. Honey will get you a whole lot farther in life than vinegar."

She turned her head to the side so that her left eye faced upward, all sign of that brief flash of fear gone. She thrashed and looked ready to shout, now that her wind was coming back. But since he had nothing at hand to stopper her mouth, he winked at her and loped off into the undergrowth, toward the south, and away from the receding sounds of random gunshots from the northern end of the canyon, the very place Julep was located.

The thought gave him brief pause, but he shook his head. You can't risk sacrificing your escape for one person, even if it is Julep, the very person who saved your life and nursed you back to health. Who tended to you with so much . . . tender devotion. No, you must move on, Slocum, he told himself. And hoping he wouldn't come across any more of Rufus's brothers—the craziest lot of settlers he'd come across in a long, long time. In a coon's age, as someone from home had said a long time ago, way back in his younger days, before the brutality of the war had changed everything for so many people, including his family—and certainly this one.

The landscape evened out, and opened up. Before him on both sides of the stream the land widened into long, grassy pastures—and in the distance he saw a sight that made his heart thump harder in his chest. Horses grazing, oblivious to the foolish men squabbling back in the little forested vale behind him.

As he made his way forward, keeping low and hustling as fast as his battered body allowed from hummock to boulder for cover, it occurred to Slocum that Deke and his vast horde of friends and relatives had probably spent their time doing this very thing forever back in the hills of Tennessee, or wherever it was they came from. If it wasn't one thing that made one branch of the family angry with another, it was something else. Whiskey or women or pigs or guns— none of it mattered in the end.

He angled down to the rushing clear stream and, bending low, scooped up handfuls of the cold water. It felt good on his sore hands, and when he splashed it on his scratched cheek, it stung, but it revitalized him, too, and seemed to lift him from his aches and worries. Here was life! Here was fresh, clean water, and there . . . horses.

He slaked his thirst quickly, and soaking the bandanna he'd had knotted about his throat, he tied it around his forehead, just above his eyes. The coolness felt good as he continued toward the horses.

The closer he drew, the more animals he saw. Hidden in another, smaller pasture off to his right, along the western edge of the stream, a half-dozen milk cows grazed, two calves lay sprawled in the sun, their big bellies making them look for all the world as if they'd been dead for days, but their lazy flicking tails told a different story.

Were there even any predators in the canyon? Just man, he thought, smiling grimly to himself. He hoped some of the horses he was approaching were broke to saddle and used to men. He didn't relish trying to make his way up and out of here on foot. He knew they rode horses in and out, for Deke had as much as admitted it to him, telling him of the crews of thieves he sent out of the canyon regularly to pillage and return to the canyon to stockpile their wares. That made this a most healthy little robbers' roost. A whole lot nicer place to live in than that unforgiving, rocky, sun-baked place Cassidy and his gang holed up in.

Before he crossed the last span of knee-high swale grass to reach the horses, Slocum hunkered low and once again checked his back trail. He thought he saw something moving behind him in the trees, so he stayed still and squinted toward the spot. Anything that might move would do so soon, he reckoned. He waited a good half minute, but saw nothing, so he turned his attention once again to the horses.

Slocum made his way slower now, taking advantage of the few seconds the nearest horse had her head down—and when she raised her head a second time, it was with perked ears. She knew something was approaching. Instinct hadn't rid her of her need for vigilance, despite the fact that the canyon didn't appear to have any predators.

He pushed through the grass, now almost on his knees, a few more feet. The big bay paused—lowered her head again. Slocum made his move forward again, but she raised her head fast, one eye on him, and nickered. The nearest horses, about eight, all raised their heads, looked her way. They looked ready and ripe for spooking. So he did the only thing he could think of. He slowly raised himself to a standing position. And though the horses tensed and seemed ready to bolt, they just eyed him.

These were broke horses, for sure. No way wild horses would have tolerated his presence this long. Hell, they'd have been halfway to China when he first emerged from the tree line.

"Whoa, girl. Whoa," he said in a low, soothing voice. He kept his eyes on hers, walked forward with a hand outstretched. A breeze lifted her forelock, danced in her long black eyelashes. Still she regarded him boldly now, turning her head in his direction. Her velvetlike nostrils flexed, working the air for sign that he was a danger. Apparently she found him to be less than threatening, for she stood still, awaiting his hand.

He had to smile because of all the creatures in this canyon, only Julep and this horse appeared to regard him more as an amusement than a danger. Two strides to go, one stride, and she walked away from him, but slowly, as if to say, "Be off with you. I was perfectly happy today until you came slinking up out of the grass. And don't think I didn't see you the entire time you approached."

"Come on, girl. Indulge me, will you? I need some help here. I could really use a guide to get up and out of this canyon full of crazies. What do you say, girl? Hmm?" And it worked. She stood still this time and he slowly made his way from her rump forward, patting her, scratching along her withers, seeing her arch slightly. This was a quiet horse, well trained, no stranger to the saddle, he bet. Probably a brood mare, given her age and disposition.

He unwound the length of greasy rope from where he'd coiled it hanging off his belt, and slowly made his way up her neck. She balked then, working her head up and down. He smelled it, too, the rope was a foul thing, slick with animal fat and wood smoke and blood and who knows what else.

"It's all we got, girl," he said and, quick as he could, fashioned a crude hackamore.

Closer to the end of the canyon, but a short ride directly before him, he hoped there would be a corral of sorts, maybe a place where they stored their tack. If not, this would have to serve.

Getting up on the horse was going to be more of a chore than he wished, for he had been a pampered, wounded man for far too long. Now he was soft, his muscles less than used to jumping and pulling. But he knew that every second he spent dithering was another second not spent getting out of the canyon, and another second that they might find out he was among the missing and come after him. Deke had to expect it. Slocum hadn't, after all, been very quiet-mouthed about his intention of leaving as soon as he was able.

And though Deke never told him he wasn't allowed to leave, the implication was that he was needed by Deke to war against the Indians and therefore he wasn't leaving. With that grim thought in his mind, Slocum grabbed a hank of the mare's mane, clucking to her as he did so, and pushing off a head-sized hummock of grass, pulled himself upward. He grasped the wide back of the horse for a handhold he knew wasn't there, hoping he wouldn't slide off. But he did.

He was cursing even as his feet slid back to the ground. Knowing the futility of trying again, for with every effort his already diminished strength would wane, Slocum looked about him for a nature-provided mounting block. And he saw just the ticket near the stream's bank. A gray boulder, large enough for him to stand atop and nearly swing a leg up and over the old girl. He led her to it, glancing back toward the northerly trees from where he'd come, and swore he saw movement once again, this time off to the east, where the trees merged with the tumbledown boulders more common at this end of the canyon, along the steep, rocky edges of the walls.

Again, he paused, sharpening his gaze on the spot. And once again, nothing appeared to move. Stop wasting time, he told himself, and led the horse to the rock. She couldn't have been more accommodating, and he half hoped she had a little more spunk, but the other horses had already loped south, pausing well away from them. Maybe they knew something he didn't about the old mare.

"Oh well, kid, seems you and me, we're operating at the same speed. Let's hope you can run faster than me, though, should it come to that." For the first time in many days, he chuckled, a wry, dry sound. But it heartened him. He might well be close to fleeing this place.

Once he'd mounted, he looked back quickly toward the trees, but saw nothing. "Spooks in your mind, Slocum," he muttered, but nonetheless hoo-raahed the horse, in a rough whisper, into an unwilling gallop southward toward the only spot he could see that might hold promise of climbing up and out of the canyon. If his guess proved to be false, he'd have to explore the entire end of the canyon, not a small task, but he had a few hours of daylight left to him, he had water, a couple of weapons, and he'd once again tasted his freedom, the thing above all others that he cherished. No man was going to take that from him. Not again.

11

The old bay mare proved as hospitable as she'd looked, and responded well, if a bit slowly, to his urgings. He roved back and forth for what seemed an eternity. He knew every minute he spent looking for something he wasn't sure existed was another wasted minute. But he had no choice. The sun was still high enough that he could see it above the western edge of the canyon. It beat down with particularly unrelenting force, and Slocum found himself missing his brimmed hat. He kept wiping his eyes with the back of his hand, readjusted the bandanna a few times, but it didn't seem to help—still the sweat ran into his eyes.

They'd made it all the way to the southwest corner of the canyon when he saw one of the reasons for the Apache's anger and refusal to give up their fight for the canyon. The remnants of an Apache burial ground lay before him, skulls smashed as if stomped by boots, others strewn about the graveled place. A slight breeze stirred aged, thin feathers still tied with bleached, curled rawhide strips to snapped lances, the wood as pitted as the bones. Scraps of blankets poked from the dirt, as if someone had spent time trying to cover up the dead with dirt, but gave up not long into the job.

Some of the bones were obviously those of children. Too many, he noted, and the puckered remains of small suits of beaded buckskin lay torn, curled, and puckered with wind, sun, and time. The entire scene looked as if it had been visited upon by a number of drunken, angry giants who had stomped the sacred place with abandon, as if such places deserved no reverence at all.

The sight set Slocum's teeth together hard, and it was all he could do to restrain himself from slipping down off the horse and making it right by restoring some sort of order, and thus dignity, to the desecrated holy site. Instead, he urged the horse to his right, turned around, and headed back the way they'd come. He would put it out of his mind, but he knew he could never forget or forgive the act. And he knew it had to be Deke's clan. Who else? Probably the trio of crazies, Rufus and her brothers.

Slocum had turned and almost reached the midpoint of the end of the canyon for a second time when the bay lowered her head and nudged to the left. He gave the horse her head—he had nothing to lose, after all—and it proved to be the right move.

She nosed between two boulders standing what seemed too close together for a man to edge between, let alone a girthy old mare. But it was the angle he'd seen them from that made them look that way. And as soon as they entered between the boulders, the sunlight's glare was cut in half and Slocum was able to see a well-trod trail, part gravel, part churned soil, and wide enough for two or three horses to walk side by side. It led upward for a few dozen yards at a gentle slope, before switching back at a westerly angle. He guessed that happened all the way up to the rim. He sure hoped so.

He was in for another surprise before they got to that first turn in the trail, though. To his left sat just what he'd suspected, a natural space in an open-topped grotto of sorts in the rock wall, just large enough to use as a small corral. The front of it was barred with three poles, currently leaning in the dirt, holding nothing in or out. To the side, a lean-to with a short, angled roof, shingled with layers of brush and branches, protected a long wall affixed with pegs, on which rested proper tack. He saw a few saddles, blankets, and bridles, and guided the old horse over to them.

She seemed familiar with the setup and stood quietly nosing the tack.

"Wish I had a carrot for you, old girl. But if things work out, I'll see to it you get a good feed before too long." He laid a blanket on her broad back, selected a saddle, cinched it on, and she gave him no trouble, then he slipped on a bridle. The entire time, he worked as fast as he could, hoping to get on up and out before his absence was noticed. He expected to find crazy rebels dropping down on him from rocky crevices at any moment. But so far none showed up.

He used the slanted rails as a ladder of sorts to help boost himself up onto the horse. Once settled, he wedged one boot into a stirrup, tugged her to the right to head on up the trail, and worked to get his other boot in the second stirrup. By then they had rounded the corner to the second angled path that he hoped would lead him up and out of the canyon.

And that was when he heard the unmistakable sound of a hammer ratcheting back into the deadliest position of all.

He raised his hands just a touch, hoping to keep his right close enough to his belt that he might be able to snatch up the big knife should he get the chance—any chance at all, in fact. Slowly, Slocum turned at the waist—could he jam his heels into the old girl and make a run for it? Probably not the wisest plan . . . yet. He saw the leading edge of a horse and rider keeping back in the shadows.

A familiar voice said, "Where I come from, that's horse theft, mister."

"Julep?"

The rider stepped forward just enough out of the shadows for light to angle across her face. "Yeah, but I reckon you knew you were being followed. For a man on the run, you sure are taking your time." She kept the Winchester rifle leveled on him. Her grip was sure, no shaking or hesitation. They were fifteen feet apart and she could easily plug him in the back, the side, didn't matter at that distance. He tried hard to not make sudden moves, the moves he wanted to make, that of jamming his heels into the mare's sides and hoping for the best. But that would be foolhardy.

Her mount looked younger, taller, more muscled. Where did she get it? Capture it in the field as he'd done, he guessed. There must have been another source of saddles stashed somewhere.

"If you'll recall, Miss Julep, I have had a rough run of it lately. Until I'm healed up, I'd venture to guess I'll be a slow mover for some time to come, eh?" His efforts at levity, if they reached her, fell flat. She didn't have a very rambunctious sense of humor, he noticed, but surely she wasn't going to side with Deke?

"Julep, I need you to let me ride on out of here. I am a free man, not anybody's prisoner—yet—and I don't intend to be kept like a camp dog, you hear me?"

"Keep talking and I'll have to cut out that silver tongue of yours. Do you hear me?"

Such hard lingo from her took him by surprise, but was that a slight quiver in her voice? Might be it was all show. "Now that's not the Julep I've come to know, the one who nursed me back to health."

Her hard gaze never wavered from his face. "And you're not the man I thought you were. If you were, you wouldn't be tucking tail and running at the first opportunity."

"What did you expect me to do, Julep? Stay here and be Deke's slave?" Slocum turned in the saddle to face her fully and relaxed his hands a bit, lowering them slightly.

Julep twitched and gripped the rifle tighter.

"Okay, okay, take 'er easy," he said, keeping his hands at chest height, where she could see them. "Let me ask you this, though. Do you know what Deke plans on doing with all those stockpiled weapons?"

Her expression didn't change much, but he sensed he'd touched on something she was unsure of. "You do know about the weapons, right, Julep?" No change in her expression, though a nerve at one eye corner jounced. Still she kept her gaze firm on him. Slocum continued, "A cave filled to brimming with enough weapons to start a war, girl. And that's exactly what he's planning on doing, Julep."

"What do you mean?" she said, almost grinning. "There ain't nobody around to start a war with—unless. Oh, you can't mean the Yankees. He swore a long time ago that he was never going to give up the fight. Ever since before the war, that's all he and, hell, all my family, women, too, ever talked about was how everybody from the North should be killed off, else they'll taint the good family stock of us Southern folk."

"But you don't agree?"

"No, as it happens, I do not agree with that. I don't like what them Yankee carpetbaggers are doing to my home. Nor do I like what they did all through the war, ruining everything in sight. But I don't wish folks any ill will. If I could just convince Deke to leave them all alone."

"I can't disagree with you, Julep, but fact is, as far as I know, at least, he's not fixing to fight the Yanks again. Not yet anyway. No, he's planning on fighting the last of that ragtag band of Apache you and your kin drove out of this canyon."

She thrust her jaw out in defiance. "You may call them ragtag, but they are a killing bunch. You saw what they did to Henry."

"Don't you think they have a right to be a little angry? After all, isn't what you and your people did to them the same as what the Yanks did to you and yours?"

"Why, it's not the same thing at all. No, not at all."

Slocum closed his eyes and sighed. When he opened

them, he said, "I don't have time for this, Julep. Look, when was the last time you came down to this end of the canyon? Been a while, has it?"

She nodded slowly, unsure of what he was driving at.

"Well, off in the southwest corner"—he jerked his chin in that direction below and to the left—"there's what's left of an Apache burial ground. A sacred place to the tribe. You know the sort of place, I can imagine way down South you all had family plots you kept tended, cleared away the creeping kudzu vine, planted flowers, maybe took a picnic lunch there and gathered with family to remember the dead."

"You bet we did," she said. "Got to honor those who came before us."

Slocum nodded. "I couldn't agree more. Which is why I found it so very sad to see that the Apache burial ground had so many babies and children in it."

"Oh," she said, touching a hand to her lips, genuine concern flitting across her eyes.

Slocum nodded. "Yeah, must have had a sickness come through. Bound to take out the small and the old first."

"What's this all got to do with me or my people?"

"Because someone—and it damn sure wasn't the Apache—tore up that sacred Apache place, ripped apart the bodies of the dead, what bones weren't scattered were smashed, stomped to bits by what looked to have been big boots." He shifted in his saddle. "Now I wonder who could have hated the Apache so much to have done that?" The old mare relaxed a rear leg and stood hipshot. She was obviously growing weary of the conversation.

"Show me," said Julep. "Show me what you're talking about. If it's true, I'll . . ."

"You'll what, Julep?"

She looked desperate, but couldn't think of a thing to say.

"I don't have time for that, Julep. You want to see it, you follow this path, fog my back trail, and you'll come upon it. Me, I have too much ground to cover and no time to do it in."

"What are you going to do?" she said, straightening in her saddle, the business end of that rifle still poking at Slocum like a menacing snake.

"I plan to head Deke off at the pass."

"What's that mean?"

"It means that I can't let him massacre all those Apache. They might have the will to stand and fight, but all those weapons would wipe them out. They're a bitter people, and there are probably more of them than you know, but even if there were a hundred, they would be no match for what Deke has planned for them."

"What can you do about it?"

"I don't know just yet. But I have to at least warn the Apache. I can't let them be massacred, not without warning. What they do with the news is up to them. I have to try, Julep." He turned around and nudged the mare with his boot heels.

"Just where do you think you're going? I'm the one with the rifle, John. Don't you forget that."

"I've wasted enough time already, Julep. If you believe what Deke's up to is the right thing, then you go ahead and shoot me in the back. But I'll not be turning around again. Good-bye, Julep." He urged the mare into a quick, for her, trot up the slow incline.

"Wait, John, they tried to kill you. What makes you think they won't try the same thing again?"

He looked back at her, but kept the mare moving forward. "They probably will."

"You'll be killed, John."

"And if I don't try, so will they—and without knowing that it's coming. That's not fair." He stopped the horse. "Julep, I was in that war, too. And I fought for the same side as your family. But I long ago had my fill of all the killing. Seems to me there's a better way of living than going around taking from people just because you want something of theirs."

"Like the canyon."

"Yep, just like that. And then not stopping there. Not being satisfied until you have taken the very last thing they have—their life—and all because you have a hate burning so deep in you that you can't recognize it's the same thing that made you so hateful in the first place." He turned once more and nudged the horse into action.

A few seconds passed before he heard a horse drawing closer. He peeked over his shoulder and saw Julep sliding the rifle into the saddle boot. "I'm coming with you."

"Oh no, you don't. As you well guessed, this thing could get ugly. I'm going alone, and with any luck, I'll get out of there in one piece. And I won't be coming back here to your cozy little canyon. But you, my dear, will be. And right now. Now turn around and go back to your own people, your own tribe. And try to talk Deke out of it. That's the best thing you can do right now."

"No. You don't know Deke. You were right, though. He's full of hurt. The Apaches, they killed his wife. He'll never be happy until they're all dead. Nothing I can say or do will change his mind. I'm only his sister, he'll never listen to me. And besides," she said, patting the rifle butt. "I'm the one with the gun. The only thing you have is that knife you took from Rufus."

Slocum's eyebrows rose. "You saw that?"

"Sure I did. I've been following you for a while now. Ever since you . . . turned tail and ran." She smirked. "Oh, I almost forgot, you have the knife in your boot, too. Right?"

It was his turn to smile. "Right as rain." He sighed. "Come on then, if you're coming. But like I said, there's no coming back. Not for me anyway."

"Same here, I reckon," she said in a quiet voice. She took a last look back down the trail toward the north end of the canyon, as if she could see through the steep rock slabs that rose all around them, obscuring her view of the verdant green land that cradled the only family she had in the world.

As they rode up the trail, heading toward yet another switchback, Slocum noticed that the passage walls appeared to be closing in, narrowing. Up ahead they met above the trail and soon they were walking forward in near-black conditions, despite the fact that it was still daylight out. Then it opened up again as suddenly as it had closed over, and they rode under a series of arches, formed who knows how many thousands of years before.

Slocum had little time to admire nature's vast engineering marvel, however, because Julep said, "Hold up a second, Slocum. You're headed toward a dead end."

He looked back to her and saw she was grinning.

"You'll like this," she said, tugging her reins hard to the left.

Then, before Slocum's eyes, she disappeared into thin air!

He didn't suspect her of trickery, but could he trust her? He didn't think he had much of a choice. Still, he touched the hilt of the big skinning knife and urged the horse forward. The rock where Julep has disappeared seemed to be a solid wall of red sandstone until he was but a few feet from it. Then, as he craned his neck to get a closer look, step by slow step the horse brought him nearer, and that's when the tall cleft opened to view. It was positioned such that unless you knew it was there, a man might ride right by the thing and not see it.

Was Julep leading him into a trap? As mysterious and surprise-filled as this canyon had proven to be, Slocum had to admit that he had no real idea how to get up and out of it. Could be she was waiting just around the bend with a whole passel of her crazy Southern rebel family and friends, ready to drag him in ropes back to the campfire and work him over, torture him for being a deserter from their bizarre cause.

And then he rounded the corner and there she was, waiting for him, a perfect circle of sunlight streaming down on her almost as if in a painting, from the round gap under a naturally formed archway in the rock trail above. And beyond that, he suspected, they weren't far from freedom.

"You had me worried," he said, glancing behind himself at the curve in the rocky path.

"Good," said Julep. "But we're not out of the woods yet. Up ahead there's another switchback, and then we'll be able to see what's in store for us."

Slocum and the mare finally made it up beside Julep. For the first time he took real notice of her mount. It was a bay mare, too, but younger, leaner. She looked spunky and fidgeted while Julep held it still.

"You sounded hesitant," he said.

"That switchback I mentioned, it's big, and one part of it is hidden from this end, making it a good place for someone to lay in wait for us."

Slocum nodded, then nudged his horse forward. "Julep, I'll need a gun. If you trust me enough to save my life, and that was before you knew me, then you should trust me now. If we're going to be ambushed, I would like some way of defending myself that levels the odds a bit." He patted the hilt of the knife. "This is a pretty impressive blade, but at a distance, it won't do as much as a bullet."

Julep hesitated, then reached behind her, unbuckled the flap on a saddlebag, and lifted out Slocum's Colt Navy in his holster. The bullet loops were filled, the leather had been oiled, and the gun even looked pretty well tended, and not too worse for the wear, considering the fall it took from the cliff top.

"Why, thank you, Julep," he said, checking the cylinder and filling it with fresh rounds. "This old gun has been with me a long time, and I'm pleased as punch to find it'll be with me awhile longer yet."

"Deke didn't want me to give it to you. Said you had to earn it."

"Yeah, well, the next few hours will likely see to that."

"We found a rifle, but it was busted up pretty bad. Figure it was that cat that did it. And the fall didn't help it none."

"Hmm," he said, strapping on his gun belt. "Didn't find a knife, not unlike this one, did you?"

"No, I didn't. Maybe Deke or one of the boys did."

"Well, I have this one now, and I'm sure it's bothering Rufus something fierce." He smiled and nudged the old mare into a walk, hugging the smooth left side of the canyon wall. "Rufus is an odd duck, that's for certain," he said in a quieter voice, keeping his eyes forward.

Julep responded in a lowered voice. "She's always been that way. Just plain odd. But we love her anyway."

"Yeah," mumbled Slocum in little more than a whisper. "There's so much about her to love."

"I heard that," said Julep, but Slocum cut her short with a raised hand of warning. He nodded forward, toward a jutting shadow. It appeared to move. He slid the Colt from its holster and eased the hammer back. Right before them, a small, furry face barely a foot off the trail rounded the corner, froze when it saw the two horses and riders.

It was a fox, and though it was obviously surprised to find them there, it regarded them for a moment before it spun and disappeared somewhere uptrail.

Slocum looked at Julep with raised eyebrows. "That bodes well—if anyone were up there, the fox wouldn't have passed this far down. As long as there aren't any places it might have sneaked in from elsewhere."

"Not that I know of," said Julep. "I think we're going to make it out of here without trouble."

"Now that's what I was wondering—just what sort of trouble are you expecting?"

"Well, I know a whole group of Deke's men went out on a job not long ago. I heard him yelling to someone about it not long before I followed you."

"How long are the men usually out on these jobs?"

"All depends, but this one . . . maybe a week or two. Hard

to say. Deke don't share much information unless you ask." She nodded toward a curve in the rock. "Behind there's what I was talking about. Could be someone back there."

Slocum thought about sliding down off the horse, realized he'd need help getting back into the saddle, but decided to risk it. He edged faster now toward the hidden space, keeping his Colt at full cock and extended, one arm braced across the other. Peering around the curve, he saw that the space was empty. "Just like the fox told us," he said.

Julep was smiling.

"How far to the top?"

"Just ahead. One more slight curve, and then we come out between two big old rocks that don't look like so much from the top. You got to know where they are to ever find your way back here."

"Then what are we waiting for?" Slocum nudged the old horse and they climbed the last bit at as fast a clip as he dared to urge the old horse. She performed admirably and soon Slocum felt the air shift yet again, reminding him of the slowly rising temperatures of the region.

The canyon would have been a tempting spot for travelers to have looked down upon, especially to people who had been trekking across near-barren wastes. With little respite from the elements, a distinct lack of water, daytime temperatures hot as blue blazes, and nights as brutal in the opposite extreme, there would be sweating and shivering in young and old alike. Slocum could only imagine what so many people had thought on seeing the canyon from above, all that lush-looking green, trees, and not just the size of a deceptive little oasis either.

This was a sunken oasis filled with the promise of a respite from the drudgery of travel, of sand in one's meager daily ration of food, of sickness and boredom and worry that they'd never make the journey. It promised relief from the real threat that they might collapse and die in the desert, their corpses scavenged by wild beasts the likes of which

most had never seen back from where they'd hailed. But
eventually they'd not find any way down into the canyon, or
would die a surprise, gruesome death at the hands of
Apache, who must have placed sentries all around the rim.

Despite his urge to get away from the canyon, that last
thought of Apache gave Slocum pause. He reined up just
short of the last few paces and held a hand up for Julep to
do the same. The devils might well be lying in wait just
outside. That was what he'd do were he an Apache forced
out of his home by Deke's people.

This time he did slip down from the horse's back. He
touched his lips with a finger, indicating to Julep that she keep
quiet. Then he crept, one slow step at a time, toward the opening in the rock. His boot heels crunched gravel and he paused,
resting his back against stone. He glanced back once at Julep,
half expecting to see her aiming the rifle at him. Or worse,
to see Deke and his band of crazy rebels filling the stone passage behind her. But there was no sign of them—no noise,
shadow, or otherwise. And of Julep, she had the rifle drawn,
all right, but had the business end aimed at the cleft in the
rock. He nodded, then shifted his attention back to the task
at hand.

Crouching even lower, Slocum slipped his sweat-soaked
bandanna off his forehead, balled it up in one hand, and
tossed it through the opening. Almost immediately, another
shadow, much like the fox's but taller, shifted slightly.

He could just see one frayed red end of the unfurled kerchief where it lay in the sand, fluttering slightly in an unseen
breeze. Now they knew he was there, and he intended to
leave. He also knew they, or at least one person—Apache
or white, that much was yet still a mystery—was out there.
He also doubted whoever it was wanted to pat him on the
back and hand him a cigar. But he'd play this hand and let
them think he was satisfied that no one caught on to his
weak attempt at "tricking" any ambushers.

He sucked in a quick breath, wishing like hell his battered body could take what he was about to dish up, and barreled through the stony cleft, low and spinning around as he made it through, hoping to see his attacker face-on. And he did.

12

Any surprise he had gained on the Apache had worn off in the time it took him to spin around. The Apache whose shadow he'd seen was almost on him, a tall, lean man with an angled face and body defined by bone and muscle, as much from the hard work of the frequent pursuit of game as it was from the lack of regular meals. But it was the man's eyes that caught Slocum's attention. They were blazing with an eager fury he'd seen earlier, when he'd fought Rufus. Here was a man whose hatred burned as bright as her own.

Slocum worked hard to step fast backward, but his muscles were weak and not limber enough to keep up with his momentum. He dug in his boot heels and pitched backward, landing on his ass with enough force to drive his teeth together hard. He shook his head and brought the pistol to bear just as the Apache lunged, a blade the equal of what Slocum had taken from Rufus held poised in a death grip, ready to chop down at Slocum's chest and gut.

There was no time to reason with the man, no time to do anything but for the animal instinct always coiled within Slocum to recognize that this angry, lunging creature was about to kill him, so he must kill it first. He touched his finger to the Colt's trigger and heard the sharp crack of a gun going off—but not the Colt Navy in his hand.

The air above him blossomed crimson, jetting fast and hot over him in a gout of Apache blood. The Indian dropped on him, already dead, his wound well placed.

Slocum jerked the hammer off the round in his gun, shoving the dead Apache off him with his other hand, and looked toward Julep. She was just lowering the smoking rifle from her shoulder when Slocum saw a leaping form dive straight at her and clean her off her horse. Another Apache!

"Nooo!" he heard Julep shout, then screams of rage from the woman echoed at him while he gained his feet. Slocum ran toward the struggling pair, a welter of flailing legs, dust, grunting, and screaming. They were too intertwined for him to shoot safely, so he jammed the Navy into his holster and dove onto what looked like the back of a young Apache.

Immediately the man bucked like a bronc and his sweaty skin proved tough to hang on to, but Slocum managed to slip an arm around the brute's neck. Biting teeth and the clawing fingers of one hand lashed at him, stinging and drawing blood. Slocum felt it well on his skin and it ignited a dormant urge to shake off the binding wraps of infirmity that had tightened about him for weeks since his unexpected drop into the canyon.

With a mighty bellow of rage, Slocum yanked hard backward, felt things inside the young man's neck tightening, then slowly giving way to his crushing choke hold.

Slocum dragged backward on the young man's body with all his strength—even while doing it, he was struck by how good it felt to work his sore muscles once again. He was only vaguely aware that Julep had stopped struggling under the man.

In his blind anger, Slocum was fully unaware of his own strength. He'd lifted the weakening Apache off the ground by the man's neck, bucking his body against his own before dropping to one knee and slamming the man's spine down on his raised knee. A cracking sound, like a muffled gunshot, yanked Slocum from his blood rage.

The Indian expelled a long, ragged sigh and sagged backward over Slocum's knee, the Apache's rough-spun cloth shirt slipping apart to reveal a thin belly arched skyward at an awkward angle. Slocum looked down at the slack-featured dead Apache, more boy than man, cradled in his arms, and shifted the body from him, lowering him to the sandy earth.

Julep! He jerked his gaze toward her and saw her lying as she had been just after the Indian had jumped at her, on her back, propped up on an elbow. She stared at him with wide eyes, her face drawn long and mouth parted, as if she were about to deny what she'd just seen. But she didn't. She merely shook her head and the horrified gaze passed from her face and settled into a mask of acceptance, as if she'd seen but another in a long lifetime's worth of horrible sights.

Slocum gained his feet and walked to her, offering a hand to help her up. But she waved him away and walked to her horse, which had come to a stop a few yards away. "You were right to kill him."

"And you, him," said Slocum, nodding toward the bloodied mess behind him. The man's blood had sprayed across Slocum's chest and the left side of his face. He looked back inside the hidden entryway to the canyon, half guessing he'd find no old mare waiting for him, that she'd returned back to the safety of the canyon and its lush grasses. But no, there she was, saddled, hipshot, and looking bored in a shaft of sunlight.

"Come on, old girl," he said, catching her reins in a bloodied hand and leading her out. He felt the numbness that always followed a killing. Even though they had had to kill or be killed, even though it was the Apache who'd put them in that position, it didn't make it any easier.

He glanced at Julep and saw she was probably feeling the same way, stunned by the moment. He knew she didn't have as much experience with killing as he did, and the thought momentarily turned his guts sour and forced a grim set to his mouth. He quelled it with thoughts of what he needed to do—which was get the hell out of there as quickly as possible. And then a second thought dogged the first— what if they were to bring the two dead Apache to the tribe? Sure, it could mean instant death, but might it also show that they were honorable, that they valued life, even if they were the ones who had taken it? The thought made sense at some deep, inner level, and yet a snort of a laugh bubbled up out of him.

"I hardly think this is an appropriate time to make wisecracks, Mr. Slocum."

He looked at her, suddenly somber. "Oh, it's 'Mr. Slocum' now, is it? Well, for your information, dearie, I was just thinking on the ethics of stealing from thieves."

"I don't know what you mean."

"I mean, I've taken a horse that doesn't belong to me, right? Not to mention this knife, the saddle, all of it. Not to mention you. Hell, I'm probably likely to be accused of kidnapping, too."

"I'm a big girl . . . John." With that, she blushed. "And there's no way I'd be here if I didn't want to be. You couldn't kidnap me if you tried."

He squinted one eye shut from the sunlight, and as he did so, he felt the Apache's blood tightening and drying on his face. "I stand corrected, Julep. Now, I'll mull over the ethics of this situation later. Right now, I have to load up these Apache on their horses."

"What horses?" said Julep. "And what did you say? Load up the Apaches?" Her eyes widened bigger than before.

"Yep." And he told her his meager plan, ending with, "So I think it's a shot at getting in their good graces. At least enough to get them to talk with me."

She pursed her lips, her eyes squinted this time, but in concentration. Finally she said, "You never actually told me what it was that you did to anger the Apaches so much that they just up and ran you off a cliff." She crossed her arms and stared at him, a mother asking a schoolchild where all the cookies had disappeared to . . .

He couldn't take more of this questioning, so he turned his attention to the two dead Apache. He dragged them side by side, laid them out in rough fashion, searched them quickly for their valuables, primarily to see if they had anything on them that might help identify them or give him some clue as to who they were, why they would attack, though he already knew the answer to that.

He was disappointed that neither of them carried anything more, weapon-wise, than a knife. He found a small, cheap steel-head ax on the ground near where the second had sprung on Julep. It must have fallen from his belt when he jumped. Slocum glanced around for hoofprints; unshod ponies would be the best they would offer. But he only saw the footprints of the bottoms of the men's bare, worn buckskin moccasins.

He glanced at Julep. Still she stared at him. He'd been biding his time, but Julep was damn persistent.

Finally he sighed. "What can I tell you, Julep? It was indeed over a young woman." He was annoyed more than anything. He'd not asked her to nurse him back to health, he'd not asked her to climb all over him when he was so weak and exhausted and probably in a stupor because of one of her homemade herbal tinctures. Hell, she was the one who ought to feel guilty, not him. And yet that blond-haired woman, those dusky eyes, the fine nose, and firm, square jaw, all atop a stunning frame, even begrimed with dirt and soiled blood, her arms, folded . . . yes, he was the one who felt the guilt.

Women, he thought to himself. Every single time I will fall for such a creature. And one day it will be the final fall, rest assured of that, Slocum old boy. He sighed, smiling to himself, and began hoisting the bloodiest Apache on the back of the old mare.

"Where are we goin'?"

He turned looked back at her, and said, "Considering you have a dead Apache draped over your horse, and so do I, well . . . how can I put this?" He smoothed the reins between his bloodied hands. "We're still going to visit your friends and mine, the Apache."

"What? After this? You saw what they're like. They'll kill us just as soon as we get in rifle shot of them."

"I'm hoping that won't happen. I have a friend among the tribe. At least I think I do. Might be she . . ."

"She?"

Slocum saw Julep's eyes narrow, watched her lead her horse right on by him. "Yep," he said. "And she's a corker, too. About so high." He held up a hand chest height, but Julep didn't look back. "Dark eyes, not a tooth in her head, and the loveliest leathery skin you ever have seen."

Julep stopped, fixed him with those narrowed eyes. "Are you telling me your so-called friend is a little old lady?"

"Could well be." Got half of it right, he thought. She's on the small side, but she's no lady, and she's not old. Just right, in fact.

"I don't believe you. In fact, I think you've lied to me about most everything since we met."

"Believe what you need to. I find it's not a bad way to make it through the day sometimes."

"John Slocum, you are a peculiar bird."

He smiled, kept walking. "I've been called worse."

They resumed their walk northward, slowly following the edge of the canyon, marked with jags of raw stone, some spiring dozens of feet into the air, much of the perimeter lined with various rock formations making it difficult to see down into the vast canyon. He suspected they were roughly equidistant to the midpoint of the canyon. So that meant that somewhere down below them, through great depths of solid rock, sat an arsenal of stolen weaponry and ammunition that would make the U.S. Army furious and not a little frightened at the same time. Any citizen with that much firepower squirreled away couldn't be up to too much good.

It would be dark in two or three hours. Slocum had hoped to make it to the Apache camp before then. Not that he knew exactly where it was, but he figured the Apache would find them soon enough. He didn't relish a night of cold camping with a woman whose loyalty he wasn't wholly sure of. Might still be that she was a ringer for her brother.

There didn't seem to be much reason or logic behind that, but it wouldn't do to let his guard down just yet. Still, she had given him his Colt Navy back. That went a far piece in convincing him that her intentions were not clouded by her crazy brother's plans.

Slocum slowly took the lead and they trudged on in silence, neither of them looking at their dead traveling companions, save to check that they weren't slowly sliding off the saddles. The horses had fidgeted for a few minutes when they'd first lashed the Apache atop them, but soon settled and grew accustomed to the pungent burdens.

The raw edge of the canyon never really revealed itself beyond the ragged tumble of boulders loosely marking it. He was tempted to climb it here and there to see if he could discern any movement down below, but decided it would gain him little knowing if Deke was rallying his troops. Of course he was. The only question now was when would they attack? The thought quickened his pace. He pushed on, picking up their dwindled pace. "We have to get at least to that rock pile at the north end of the canyon by dark."

Julep nodded, said, "Okay, then," and kept walking.

"I don't have much in the way of supplies," said Slocum with a snort. "I didn't think that far ahead. Just tried to get on out of Deke's line of fire. Do you have anything to eat in those saddlebags of yours?"

This time she did smile. "I did think of that, actually. Unlike some people, I am rarely unprepared. Especially when it comes to food. I do love to cook."

"I know you do." Slocum patted his belly. "Unfortunately there won't be any fires tonight."

"The Apaches?"

"Sort of, but mostly I was thinking that if Deke sent up a small crew to find us, well, we don't have to make it simple for them."

Julep nodded. "And then there's the big group he's expecting to return from their latest job."

"Yeah, good point. Tell me about Deke's operation, would you? What's he hope to accomplish with all this?"

There was a long silence that stretched and stretched, the edges of it taking on a decidedly frosty tone. He had just about decided she wasn't inclined to divulge her brother's secrets when she spoke.

"Deke's a complicated man, John. He's not nearly as crazy as I bet you think he is."

Slocum didn't know quite what to say to that. He did, in fact, think Deke had traveled a bit farther around the bend than most folks do. But how far, he wasn't sure.

They trudged on for a while more, each lost in their respective thoughts. Then the rocky knob that formed the north end of the canyon's rim came slowly into view like a shimmering wraith. With each step they walked, it grew larger, more impressive, until finally they were close enough that from his angle he could make out parts of the rock face where he'd emerged, after climbing up from the other side, the spots where he'd fought the snake and the lion. And then the Apache. There were a few spots along the rim where he could glimpse down into the canyon, and it looked like a long way down. No wonder he still had a headache.

They made it to the base of the rock pile just as the sun touched the ragged mountain peaks far to the west. Maybe this was all a mistake; maybe they should have ridden south or west, just kept going until they hit Mexico or California and the ocean. But what Deke had in mind for the Apache and the Bluebellies had to be stopped.

If he could convince the Apache to send him and a couple of men back into the canyon to blow up the arsenal, they might well avoid all such trouble, rendering Deke and his men toothless and unable to do much more than stamp their feet. It was a long shot, but it was all he had to try.

After a cold but tasty meal of flaky biscuits and bacon—Julep had cooked up a mess of it that morning—they agreed to take turns keeping watch. Slocum insisted Julep sleep first, though he had a hard enough time doing so. She was a feisty woman, no doubt, and one that no matter how hard he tried, no matter how beaten down he still felt, could still spark something inside him.

He'd watched her retrieving the tasty grub from her bags, bent over and swaying unintentionally before him as though humming to herself or considering some deep reason or other why she was doing what she was doing. And it was a fine sight.

But that had been more than two hours before. Given all they had been through in the past little while, he had no intention of bothering her once her head hit the rocky pillow. She was, if possible, even more attractive in sleep. Even with no soft bed and nobody for company but a couple of dead Apache who had wanted nothing but to kill her mere hours before. And she was escorted by a man still recovering from serious injuries. He wasn't afraid of dozing off, knowing she had placed her trust in him. He had to make sure he earned it.

He sat there in the dark, the two dead Apache stiffening up a few yards away, the horses picketed as close as he dared, both of them standing hipshot and almost leaning against each other. Julep made a few light breathing noises—the only women he'd ever heard offer up mouth-wide snores were prostitutes. Not all of them, just a few of the lustier, more hard-drinking gals he'd come across.

He was doing his best not to think about what he was going to do when they were found by the Apache, what they were going to do when the Apache decided not to listen to him. In such situations, Slocum knew he had to count on the worst happening, while hoping for the best. But in his experience, hope was a waste of time. He hadn't counted on having to drag along a sidekick, much less a woman. And he definitely hadn't counted on having his hands full with two dead Apache. But he'd give them high marks for their bravery, if not for their timing and lack of suitable weapons.

In the dark, he glanced toward their laid-out bodies, not seeing much. One was especially young. God, but he hated that he'd had to kill the lad. Slocum wondered if the boy had ever been kissed.

In the daylight, when they'd attacked, they looked thin, less robust than they ought to. This he blamed on them being kicked out of their fertile canyon. Those people had every right to be angry with the whites. And the more Slocum thought about it, the more he realized his plans were shot full of holes. He groaned and whispered, "Idiot," to himself. Being caught with two dead Apache would not bode well for them. Not at all.

Despite his earlier thinking about essentially turning themselves over to the mercy of the Apache in hopes of explaining their dire situation before the Indians could kill them, the foolishness of this plan only now occurred to Slocum. He knew that Julep's hesitation had been more right. She had been trusting her gut instincts, while he was merely thinking without thinking. What was wrong with him lately? And what was wrong with Julep that she would not press the issue more with him?

And that was when he heard soft, padding sounds, lots of them, as if they overlapped—that probably meant many people, Apache, he'd bet, cat-footing in skin-soled shoes. Slocum remained motionless, save for his thumb slowly pulling back on the Colt's hammer. Whoever it might be was coming up fast and trying to be quiet. Slocum was pleased he had decided to sit on a low wedge of rock rather than on the ground. From this perch, with solid rock behind, he could launch himself forward a hell of a lot easier than he could if he were sitting on the ground.

He bent forward ever so slightly, checking, and felt the reassuring heft of the bone-handled skinning knife as it pressed against his gut from its spot wedged into his belt. Good, he had a feeling he'd soon need it. And the boot knife, he knew, was also tucked in where it should be. Too late to nudge Julep awake. He could barely see her in the dark, but hoped that meant she'd also be unseen by whoever was approaching.

As he sat there, ears straining to detect the sounds he'd detected, he heard them change, peel apart in at least two directions, maybe more. They were splitting up into smaller groups, surrounding them. Despite their precautions about not starting a campfire—on a plain such as this, a fire would be seen for quite a distance—he and Julep had been found. And probably by the Apache.

Slocum heard the faster approach in the dark, off to his right. To his left, the soft sounds changed, spaced apart, then he heard a grunt. Someone was climbing the boulders to his left, up behind the still-sleeping Julep, probably getting set to spring at them. The same measured steps came at him from in front. Slocum gauged that the one on his right would be on him first, then it was anyone's guess if the one in the rocks to the left would be second, or the one in front. He'd worry about them when the time came.

And then he knew that time was upon him.

The uneven scuffing sounds suddenly stopped. Slocum bent low, pivoting at the last second away from where he'd been seated, and tucked into a roll onto his right shoulder. He caught a quick sight of a lunging shape and, too late to grab for the knife, touched his finger to the worn trigger of his Colt Navy. The death-dealing barrel barked its hard oath loud, stabbing the night with flame and sending the attacker into a mad, spinning dance, screaming and flailing as if he'd gobbled peyote all day long.

Slocum didn't have time to inspect the flopped, thrashing man, because he knew there were at least two others coming in fast.

By then, Julep had screamed and crawled tighter to the base of the big rock she'd been sleeping beside. The horses lunged and thrashed in a frenzy, unable to do much more than whinny and slam into each other. Slocum kept rolling up off his shoulder, all signs of his ailments gone as his body slid, like an oiled machine, into old familiar poses—one arm up, skinning knife clenched tight, the other extended, a fresh round chambered and cocked. He rolled up onto one knee just as the next brute dove out of the darkness.

Then he heard Julep yelp, and glanced quickly in her direction—there was another form atop her, or she on it, he had no way of knowing. What he'd give for a lantern. But then he had no more split seconds to spare. As he drove his knife arm forward, the oncoming attacker must have seen it, for he lunged to one side and Slocum's blade barely found purchase. But a howl of pain arose beside him in the dark. It was a howl that devolved into what sounded like someone grunting, "Goddammit, I been gutted!" And this was not in the Apache tongue.

"Julep!" shouted Slocum. "You okay?" But then the one who'd attacked him jumped on his back and a wet fist slammed into his head, once, twice, as he sliced upward with the skinning knife, tried to land a killing jab. He raised the Colt, aimed it above and behind himself, and just as he settled his forefinger on the trigger, the revolver was snatched from his hand.

"Well, what have we got ourselves here?"

The person who did the snatching was the one who spoke. The man on Slocum's back groaned, but managed to keep Slocum somewhat immobilized, though he still struggled. Then the man who took his gun tapped Slocum hard on the temple with the barrel and said, "Nah, nah, nah, that ain't how this is going to play. You got me? You hold yourself still or I'll tell Lemuel there to gut you like you done to him."

"He got me bad, Shin. Done shot me, then sliced me! I need help."

This came from the man sitting on Slocum's back. Slocum did not utter a "thank you," though he would have liked to have jammed an elbow—and then a knife—in the man's face. But that was sort of difficult when the business end of his own Colt Navy revolver was jammed in his eye.

It sounded as if the man holding the gun was busy doing something, rummaging in a pocket maybe. And then he thumbed a match alight, close by Slocum's face. The man had leaned down and stared at him from inches away. As the match flared, its quick orange glow illumined the sunken-cheeked, gaunt face of a tall, thin man with dark eyes, bushy brows that pinnacled in the middle, above each eye, so much so that the man looked like some sort of political drawing in a newspaper.

When he opened his mouth, Slocum saw craggy spots lined with stumpy black teeth where a full set had long before resided. They looked painful and made Slocum's own well-tended choppers itch in sympathy.

Despite the man's haggard appearance, Slocum didn't think he was much more than thirty-five, maybe forty or so. He'd probably taken the hard road around the barn, met up with a grizzly or three, and somehow lived to tell the tale.

"Mort, you get off that one there and light up them lanterns."

"Shinbone? Is that you?" said Julep.

She sounded as if she was unhurt, and for that Slocum was grateful. For everything else, he was just plain ticked off.

"Why, Julep dear, is that you, honey? I had no idea." The tall man Julep had called "Shinbone" didn't sound surprised in the least. "I do declare, you run into the funniest situations out here in this forsaken hell of a place."

"Shinbone, thank God. You've mistaken us for someone else. We're . . ."

"Yes, honey? You're what?"

Slocum shrugged hard, as he suspected that the man atop him, the one he'd wounded, wasn't paying attention. He was right, and his efforts were rewarded with a howl of pain from the bastard. Slocum rolled to one side, half expecting the Colt to deliver a killing flash in the dark camp. But the man called Shinbone just laughed.

"Lem, get your mangy ass off him. If you're going to bleed and whimper, then get yourself off to that rock over yonder and let Mort in there tie up this rascal. That is, if Mort will get on the stick and get them lanterns lit."

"I'm gettin' them, boss. It ain't easy luggin' all this here gear."

"You should have thought of that before you ran our packhorse to death yesterday morning." To Slocum, Shinbone said, "Not so fast there, rascal man." He rapped Slocum on the bean again with the snout of the revolver. "You and me, we got things to chat about."

"Shinbone," said Julep, coming closer. "He's okay, he's with me."

Just then, the other man, Mort, mooched and clanked into dim view, carrying a dirty canvas pack loaded with gear.

How did I not hear that contraption of a man approaching? thought Slocum. Unless they've been tucked away into these boulders close by the entire time we were here . . .

Mort set down his load with a clanking thud and a groan, then hurried to light a lantern. It bloomed with the touch of a match, and Slocum looked up from being nearly facedown in the dirt. For the first time, he took in the scene around him. He saw Shinbone, and yes, the man was tall and crazy looking. There was Julep, on her knees off to his left, looking confused. Her hands were raised to her mouth, and she looked at Shinbone with wide eyes, as if he were a demon she had just locked eyes with.

The pack mule man named Mort was as Slocum thought, a short, dumpy little character with a bubble of white belly poking through his busted-button flannel shirt.

As if in response to Slocum's thoughts of a few seconds before, Shinbone spoke. "Been eyeballin' you two pretty near since you crawled on up outta that canyon—ahead of you, of course. Surprised the hell out of us, I tell you what."

He spit and grinned. "Mort, you don't tie up these two in lickety-split fashion, well, you and me, we're going to have a good, old-fashioned set-to, right here and now. You catch me?"

"Yeah, yeah, all right, Shin. You got it. Just lemme free up some of this here hempen rope." The fat man fidgeted and finally freed a coil of scratchy-looking rope from the side of his laden pack.

Shinbone sighed, adjusted the Colt when Slocum shifted his elbows. "Easy, mister. I got me a craving to kill and you could well be the cure."

"Shinbone! I told you he's with me!" Julep glared at him and began rising to her feet.

"You don't set right back the way you was, sweet Julep, and I will kill this knob-headed sumbitch right here and now!" Shinbone's voice rose to a shout.

Slocum felt the tip of the Navy's barrel dig into his face. He gritted his teeth and said, "Julep. Stay put. We'll get this figured out soon enough."

"Now, see?" Shinbone jammed the barrel into Slocum's temple even deeper.

Slocum clenched his teeth until he was sure they would collapse in a cloud of fine powder.

Shinbone spit and continued, "I don't recall giving you permission to open your foul mouth, But if I did, by all means"—he jammed the barrel harder and Slocum went with it so his neck wouldn't snap—"feel free to keep jawing if I am in the wrong." He waited a few seconds, then said, "No? Good, I suspect you are a wiser critter than I give you credit for. But the night is young and there is still time for you to prove me wrong. Which I suspect will soon happen."

Julep let out a low sob. Shinbone fixed her with a glare and a sneering smile. She clamped a hand over her mouth, her eyes watery with welling tears.

"Don't tell me you got something to say, too, dearest Julep?"

Trembling, she shook her head as Mort gently pulled her hand from her mouth and bound her wrists behind her back.

"Good. Now stop interrupting my story, y'all. Where was I? Oh yeah, see, me and the boys, we was fixing to mosey on down into the canyon, tell ol' Deke what we found for him on our last little foray, when what do we see a-squirmin' around near the entrance to the canyon?"

Mort finished tying Julep's wrists and commenced to do the same to Slocum.

Shinbone prattled on. "I don't have to tell you, Julep darlin', that seeing anything near them rocks what mark the entrance is a shock and a half, ain't it?" He grinned at her, and received a tearful glare in return.

His smile dropped as fast as a hot kettle from an ungloved hand. "I said, 'Ain't it?'" A long, grimy hand lashed out, caught Julep across the left cheek. Her head snapped to the side, and she uttered a low moan of pain.

"Next time, you answer me, you hear?"

Slocum could see her fighting back tears.

"That's enough, you filthy animal," growled Slocum, struggling to stand. "You itchy for a fight? I'll oblige you. Drag your sorry ass over here."

It worked. Shinbone spit another long stream of chaw juice to the side. It spattered on a rock.

"I reckon you think you're a tough nut, huh, friend?" said Shinbone.

"I have plenty of friends, and you aren't one of them,"

said Slocum, continuing to work his fingertips down into his boot top. He'd nearly been there when Shinbone had smacked Julep, now he had the fool's attention, but he wasn't quite ready for him. He needed another minute to slip the knife free and slice through the poorly tied ropes wrapped around his wrists.

But Shinbone surprised him. He lashed out with one of those long legs, and the toe of his boot caught Slocum under the chin.

"John!" shouted Julep.

A blast of hot sparks flowered before his eyes, seeming to light up the night. He struggled to remain upright, but found he'd already sagged to the ground, once again his face pressed hard to the dirt.

He felt someone else kicking him in the back and laughing. Must have been that worthless one he'd grazed, then sliced in the side. He'd forgotten about him.

"Lay off of that, Lemuel! He's mine." Shinbone barked the order and bent low, his long, bony face inches from Slocum's, who tried to force himself up out of the dirt. But the tall man shook his head, saying, "Uh-uh-uh, you stay right there," and pushed down on Slocum's upturned shoulder.

He spoke in a low, gravelly voice that slid from between his lips like a snake gliding over a hot rock. "Gonna have us some fun . . . John." Then he laughed, long and loud, still staring at Slocum. His breath gouted in Slocum's face, stinking and sour of coffee, whiskey, old greasy food, and the rot from his stumplike teeth. Tobacco juice marked the lines and creases on either side of the man's mouth, and a thin stream of it glistened on his chin.

"Any more fun like that," said Slocum, struggling to stop the foul vision of the man's face before him from spinning more than it was, "and I'll have to decline your kind offer."

Shinbone's brow wrinkled up for a moment, and he leaned back, one hand rubbing his chin as if he were considering some deep thought. "I don't rightly know what such fancy words mean, but I can tell you"—he held up a long finger in the air, surprise writ large on his face—"that I have about had enough of every single thing about you."

He stood and slid Slocum's pistol from his belt, hefting it as if weighing it with his hand. "Nice piece. And it will serve its purpose well. You see, as I was saying, there ain't a reason in the world why I shouldn't up and shoot you in the head like any right-thinking man would do to a hydro-phoby dog."

"No!" shouted Julep. "No, no, don't, Shin. He didn't mean nothing by that. He was just defending me, that's all. Harmless. He's harmless."

"Now," said the tall man, not looking at her, "that there is what I'm talking about. You see how you got my lady love, my dove, all a-flustered? Why, before you come along, I reckon we was closer than a couple of weevils in a boll. Now, though, what do I find on my return from fighting the enemy through forest and fen?" He warmed to his topic and Slocum took the opportunity to use his head and his right arm, which was under him, and his shoulder, to push upward once again, and try to at least gain a sitting position.

But Lemuel had other plans and landed another kick squarely on Slocum's back. Right beside his spine. He groaned, lost his breath. The kick hurt like the devil was sizzling his hide with a hot brand.

"Dang it all, Lemuel, what did I just get finished saying? Don't you have enough to worry about without pissing me off? Here, if holding your own guts in ain't trouble enough for you, maybe this will keep you occupied." In one swift movement, he raised the Colt Navy, thumbed that hammer back, and squeezed that trigger.

Slocum heard the man behind him slam hard into the rocks. Just in his line of sight, he saw one leg quiver, spasm, then come to rest.

"Oh, you bastard! You killed Lem! Oh, Shin, how could you kill your own kin?" Julep had gained her feet by then and rushed at the tall man in a wild rage. She had her head down and slammed into his chest, but he was ready for her and her blow barely rocked him on his heels. He held her by the shoulder and, laughing, reached down and kissed her on the mouth. She spit at him and whipped her head side to side, struggling to get out of his grasp. He obliged her by pushing her roughly.

Her legs couldn't keep up with her momentum and Julep tripped, sprawled backward, and Slocum saw her head hit the ground, bounce, then she was still. "Julep!" He struggled once again to rise and this time managed to get to his knees. "You bastard. If she's hurt . . ."

"You'll what? You ain't got a trick up your sleeve, mister. Now just set right there and keep your trap shut while I finish my story. As I was saying before all these assholes interrupted me, I seen you early on, and seen how you made quick work of them Apaches yonder." He nodded toward the two corpses.

"And I said to myself, Shinbone, you got to watch that one. He's a sidewinder if there ever was one. And then I up and find you been slipping something to my woman. So I tell the boys, why don't you two come with me, we'll see what's what, how all this is playing out with Julep and this stranger. We'll get to the canyon in due course, but right now, I need to see what I'm thinking I'm seeing." He looked down at Slocum. "You understand me, boy?"

"Get on with it, fool."

That struck a nerve once again with Shinbone. I gotta stop doing that, thought Slocum. At least until I get this boot knife working. He knew it was his only chance, especially since Shinbone had just shot one of his own relatives and laid Julep out cold—or worse.

The tall oaf smiled, nodded, and said, "So we watched you and Julep, but you disappointed me, 'cause you didn't find her to be in the mood, if you know what I mean."

"I suppose I do. You're telling me you like to watch other people as they buck in the saddle, is that it?"

Shinbone once again lost his smile. "I about have had enough of you and your confounded interruptions." He raised the Colt, and grinned. Tauntingly, he lifted his big, flat thumb and rested it atop the hammer.

Slocum worked the boot knife faster than ever, but in the fraction of a second that it took to stare down the tall man, he realized there was no way he was going to make it, because Shinbone had proven to have a short fuse and could only be pushed so far.

As Slocum's fingertips worked to raise the knife from his boot, then close around the hilt, he continued to stare at the man, square in the eyes. After all his adventures, if this was the way he was going to go out, then dammit, he was going to go out with a fight.

He dug his left boot toe into the soft sandy ground beneath him; the right he'd already braced against a boulder. He didn't have time to cut through the rope wraps. But he gripped the small knife's handle firmly and with a growl drove himself forward, straight at Shinbone's shins, covering the man-length of space in a heartbeat of time.

It had the hoped-for result of catching the tall man by surprise. Shinbone shouted, "Whaaa?" and buckled backward.

The two men slammed hard to the ground, Slocum landing atop Shinbone. He had hoped the man would have dropped the revolver when he fell, but he felt its heavy thudding weight batter him on the side of the head as Shinbone flailed and slammed at him.

Slocum could only grip the small knife tight in his blood-engorged hand from the poorly tied but too-tight rope. He hoped he didn't drop it and not even know, so bad were his hands throbbing. He ground his teeth together tight and with his already pounding head battered the thin man in the chest, the ribs, the arm, and working his way upward, he drove a knee into the man's crotch. Again and again, using whatever he could for leverage. Then with a downward slam of his head, he pounded his forehead into Shinbone's face.

Just what he'd hoped for—Shinbone's nose crunched sideways, smearing in a pulpy spray against the side of his face, and he howled like a gut-shot coyote. All his flailing stopped and he tried to speak through a bubbling wad of thick, bloody phlegm. Then his face sagged to one side and he lost consciousness.

Slocum tried to breathe, found he was so winded it didn't feel as if he'd ever pull in another breath. He grunted, raising his head, and blinked several times. He scrunched his eyes shut tight, trying to blink away the blood, opened them, and blinked. Couldn't be—he thought he saw a man standing before him. Good God, were there more of Shinbone's cohorts?

Slocum tried to speak, but only managed a raspy cough. He looked again and saw a ring of men before him, all standing a good dozen feet away, just at the ring of firelight, staring at him. They were Apache.

He closed his eyes again and righted himself, then rolled from atop Shinbone and onto his back in the dirt. He wasn't sure he was still clutching the boot knife. He hoped he hadn't dropped it, but his hands were so numb from being bound that they felt like they were each holding a bag of bees. And where was the Colt? It had been in Shinbone's right hand, then Slocum had landed the nose-breaking head move and the man had sagged. So the gun must be somewhere beneath him in the dirt. He worked to scrabble for it, hoping to locate it before . . .

He looked up and saw a leg clad in torn peasant trousers, much the same as Mexicans wore. A bare foot with gnarled toes and horned with calluses reached in the dirt beside him and kicked at something. Slocum jerked his head and followed it with his eyes. It was his Colt. Damn. Hopefully they hadn't seen the boot knife. Hopefully he still had it.

"You . . . crazy man."

Slocum looked up again, squinting through a sticky matte of blood in his eyes. He scrunched his eyes tight together, then opened them. "Who said that?" he said, eyeing the still-staring Indians.

"I," said a broad-chested man in a striped shirt, with dark hair cut raggedly that hung nearly to his shoulders. He thumbed himself in the middle of that massive chest. "I say this."

"Glad to hear it. What's the plan, then?" It was all Slocum could do to hopefully distract this man enough to at least get the knife back in his boot. He knew that with this many Apache watching him, there was no way he could slice through his wrist wrappings, then take them all on.

The man who had spoken made a few hand gestures, spoke softly into the ear of a man beside him, looking at Slocum now and again as he did so. Finally the man receiving the instructions nodded and beckoned to two more Apache. They approached Slocum. He had just enough sensitivity in two fingertips that he felt he still had the small knife. He scrabbled to jam it back in his boot just as the three men bent low over him and flipped him over, then dragged him facedown, toward the man who had spoken.

"You . . . I have seen you another time."

It wasn't much of a question. Then Slocum guessed he must have been one of the Apache who'd chased him that day weeks before, forcing him into the high rocks.

One of the Apache swung a dark, meaty hand hard and fast, catching Slocum across the jaw. It stung, but he righted his face and managed to stare down the offender. "You do that again and I will not take it kindly."

The warning fell on confused ears. The man's quizzical look almost forced a smile from Slocum. But not quite. Then the broad-chested man spoke again. "You . . . stop your talk. We"—he gestured with his hand held flat in front of him, arching it back and forth as if he were polishing a flat surface—"we are the ones who talk first, then you answer. You do not make threats." He waited a moment for that to sink in, then he pointed a meaty finger at Slocum. "Now. You—tell me what happened here."

13

What could Slocum say? If he started from the beginning, he'd all but admit he was cavorting with the chief's daughter, a sure death sentence. And who would believe that he'd tangled with a lion, Apache, snakes, then fell from the high rocks down into the canyon, and lived. And then was nursed back to health by Julep—there his attention diverted back to her. He hoped she was just unconscious.

"Help her!" growled Slocum. The man who'd cracked him across the face before poised to do so again, but the broad-chested man—perhaps he was a chief?—stayed his hand and spoke to him in a low flurry that was less than kind, Slocum was pleased to note.

The man set his jaw hard, but nodded his assent. He glared once down at Slocum, then turned and strode to Julep. He lightly slapped her face, and Slocum was pleased to note the man seemed almost gentle. Perhaps it was because as a white woman, Julep might be considered by this brave as a coup of sorts, a fine trophy to add to his stable of wives. There were worse fates, he decided, and at least it would keep her alive should they try—or succeed—in killing him.

I can't go thinking like that, he thought. Then he heard a groan and all eyes fixed on Shinbone. "Ohhh . . ."

The tall, stump-toothed man was coming around. If he came to, anything he might say could potentially harm what Slocum had been thinking of telling the Apache. Only one thing to do.

Slocum pushed up onto one side, pivoted on his hip, and within seconds delivered a quick heel kick to Shinbone's head. The man's groaning stopped, his head whipped back, and his eyelids fluttered. For a second, Slocum wondered if maybe he'd kicked too hard and killed the jerk.

"Why you do that?" The broad-chested man aimed his mighty furrowed brow down at Slocum.

"Because . . . he is a killer and a thief and I don't much like either." Hardly eloquent, but it would have to suffice. The big fellow appeared to be mulling this over. If he'd had a beard, he'd probably be stroking it in long, luxurious swipes, while he let his mind wrestle with the problem of what to do with the crazy whites before him. All this time, other than the ones commanded to do his bidding, the other ten or so Apache men still stood in a semicircle just at the fringe of the lamplight.

Finally the man spoke. "Why that one"—he gestured at the lolled Shinbone—"do all these bad things?" Then another hurried thought appeared to have nipped at the heels of that first one, for he followed it with a second. Bending low, his great wrinkled brow drove his eyebrows together in concern. "Why I know you not do these things? Maybe, huh?" He fluttered his hands in a gesture that imitated "maybe" as well as any creature could.

Slocum licked his lips and looked toward Julep. She had slowly come around and her eyelids fluttered, her voice came to her, and she moaned. He was thankful that she was awake. And he hoped that seeing the Apache wouldn't do something to her that he did not anticipate. He had no idea how any one of the whites from the canyon would react to realizing they'd become a captive of the Apache when they were caught. He was also afraid that she might do something to foul his still poorly formed plans. He had to head off any trouble at the pass.

"Julep! Hey, Julep! It's John. Over here, girl. That's right. You okay? Focus now, we'll be fine. These men came along just in time, saved us from Shinbone and the others. We are lucky they did, girl. You hear me? Julep?"

She moaned softly, and the Apache pushed her blond hair from her forehead. She flinched at the gesture and looked at him for the first time, realizing someone was that close. She screamed, a short, clipped sound that Slocum barked a quick command to try to stop. It worked.

"Julep, dammit, girl. Did you hear what I said? These men came along, saved us from that bad man, Shinbone. You hear me?" He hoped his wide eyes and gritting teeth didn't give away his desperation to the broad-chested Apache leader.

Julep slid her eyes from the staring Apache beside her to Slocum. She nodded after a few seconds, then looked back at her close captor.

The broad-chested Apache toed Slocum's shoulder and he looked up at the man. "I ask you why you not the one who do these things." He waved his hand broadly and Slocum knew his callused hand's gesture had taken in the two dead Apache.

Slocum looked at Broad Chest, as he came to think of him, convinced that the man was indeed a chief, perhaps the tribe's sole chief. The thought made his gut tighten. But the two men stared into each other's eyes. Finally, Slocum spoke. "I never said I wasn't the one. Just that he's a bad, bad person. Not someone I trust. Not someone we call friend." With that he jerked his head toward Julep, who sat watching the exchange with mounting horror in her eyes. He wondered if she'd ever come face-to-face with her sworn enemy, or rather Deke's sworn enemy. The Apache. Make that one of his sworn enemies. The man seemed to have a pocket full of lists of people he felt were evil and should be dealt with. Apparently with his growing arsenal of firepower.

"Why you here?" said Broad Chest.

"I will admit it's a right odd situation to find in the desert like this." Slocum licked his lips. "Any chance I can sit up, get a swig from that canteen, and tell you properly?"

Broad Chest canted his jaw, regarded Slocum with squinted eyes. "Yes, but no untie hands. You still mine." He jerked that wide thumb at his chest again. Slocum began to see that was a favored gesture.

"All right, then. But please give the lady a drink first. She has been through a lot and it's not been easy nor fair to her."

Julep snorted, and Slocum knew she was fine. Leave it to her to find something to be irate about at a time like this.

Broad Chest looked at Julep, then back to Slocum. "She no like this plan."

Slocum swore he saw a smile flit like a moth across the man's dark face. Then it was gone, replaced with the stony glare once again.

He was helped to a sitting position and stretched his legs out in front of him, with his back leaned against a rock. It felt good to flex his leg muscles. He glanced down at Shinbone, but the man was still out of it. Good. "Now, Chief— may I call you 'Chief'?" Slocum was taking a big risk in using the term, but he felt pretty sure the man was not your average brave.

Broad Chest nodded once, but he noticed a few of the men beside him flinched, noticed a raised eyebrow here and there. So this one might not be the chief, after all.

"We, the girl and I, are from . . ." Here we go, point of no return, thought Slocum. "We are from down there. He jerked his head back behind him. This caused no reaction at all from the assembled men. Curious. He continued. "And we have very important news to tell you." He waited a few heartbeats, then with no reaction, he continued, "Very important information for you, the Apache."

They were definitely his audience now. Much like that half-naked puppeteer woman from Paris, France, had had the entire crowd at the Birdcage in Tombstone spellbound by her antics. And even more so once she'd gotten drunk and had fallen into the crowd. What a glorious mess.

"You tell us or we kill you now, you understand?" Broad Chest had obviously lost his patience.

"The news is . . . only fit for the ears of the chief of the Apache."

As the meaning of his words occurred to the Indian, Slocum watched a mask of rage take shape on the man's face. The broad-chested man's meaty hands clenched and unclenched, he showed his full set of white teeth, stark in the dim glow of the lamp light. He whipped his wide face from Slocum to Julep and the fat gear carrier. Then down at Shinbone, and finally back to Slocum. "Kill them all. Now."

That was not what Slocum had hoped would happen. But at least now he knew the man was not a chief. "Hey, now, fella. That's not the brightest move you'll make all day, I can tell you that. What's your chief going to say when he's denied the knowledge I have, information that could save all the lives of your people."

"Bah! Kill him now!" He thrust a thick finger at Slocum and then dragged it across his own throat and smiled, a wide leering thing.

The nearest Indian slipped a broad-bladed knife from his belt. He, too, grinned as if this was the most fun he'd have all year. And it would probably be just that, thought Slocum, struggling to gain his feet. But the man was on him in fingersnap speed. "I can guarantee you the canyon. You will have it back, all of it, if you spare us."

Broad Chest scowled, then held up a hand and barked an order—one word—in Apache. The man with the knife beside Slocum paused. He looked perturbed that his fun was once again interrupted.

"Leave him alive. The others, kill."

"No!" shouted Slocum, getting up on one foot, resting his weight on one knee, ready to spring. "You kill them, you might as well kill me, too, because I won't talk, no matter how much of your Apache torture you practice on me. And then you'll never know if I was telling the truth or not. I'm saying it plain, I know of a way for you to drive the whites out and get your canyon back."

"Forever?" said Broad Chest.

Slocum raised his eyebrows and shrugged his shoulders. "That's not up to me. That all depends on how much effort you Apache put into defending it. But it seems to me if this"—he nodded toward the man with the knife—"is the quality of the warrior you have, then you might as well quit now, go back to grubbing with the women for roots and berries."

Broad Chest looked briefly at the knife-wielding man, then at Slocum. And the fake chief actually smiled. "You speak truth, even though it might kill you. That is good. I take you—all of them—to see our chief." He turned to his men, who had for the most part remained silent, staring at the whites with sullen, scowling looks as if they were regarding a gut pile alive with writhing worms.

From out of the dark behind them, a younger Indian led two horses.

"Hey," said Mort, the fat man, speaking for the first time since the Indians' arrival. "Them are our horses—Shin's and Lem's anyway."

"Shut up!" hissed Julep.

None of the exchange seemed to bother the Indians. They acted as if the whites weren't even there, but Slocum knew from much past experience with quiet Indians that they took everything in, revealed little about themselves. Most of them, he was convinced, knew English better than he knew their lingo.

Another Apache retrieved the horses Slocum and Julep rode, and began loading the two dead Apache across the backs of one horse as if they were of as little consequence as a sack of flour. Broad Chest kicked Shinbone in the side and the tall white groaned. The Indian grunted something at one of his men and two of them dragged Shinbone to another horse, draped him across the saddle, and tied his wrists to his ankles under the horse with rawhide thongs.

All the while, the sky to the east had begun shading from black to gray to a subtle deep purple hue. The slow dawning day had begun to cast just enough light that, combined with the lanterns' glow, Slocum could take a good look at their captors. Their faces were still muted by shadow, but they definitely were some of the men who had chased him weeks before on this very plain.

He wondered if they had his Appaloosa and gear. It was probable—there was no way they'd leave a perfectly good horse and useful gear in the rocks. And since they'd seen him ride in there with him, then fall into the canyon, they darn sure knew he wasn't coming back for his possessions. He suspected they were taking them to their camp, so he'd find out soon enough.

One of the Indians kicked the fat man in the ass and he squealed and pitched forward, facedown in the dirt. The Apache laughed, all but Broad Chest. He bellowed something in Apache that made them all shut up as quickly as they had started. While the fat man was still on the ground, one of the Indians dropped down onto his back with one knee, jamming the breath from his lungs.

"Is that necessary?" shouted Julep, staring hard at Broad Chest, who nodded toward her, then Slocum, indicating she should knee-walk over beside him.

"Julep, let it go," said Slocum in a low voice. "We need

to pick our battles now, and this isn't one of them. He'll be fine." They both looked at Mort grunting and writhing under the Indian's knee as the brute tied the fat man's hands tight behind his back with leather thongs.

"What's his story anyway?" said Slocum to Julep, nodding toward the fat man.

"Mort's harmless. Good enough fella, but for some reason has always thought the sun rose and set with ol' Shinbone."

"Speaking of good ol' Shin, what's his story?"

"What do you mean?"

"I mean, is he a trusted ally of Deke? And what was he doing spying on us?"

"You don't think it could be because of me?" Julep didn't sound as if she was joking.

"No, but I'm curious to know why he's out here, afoot, and shouting and lighting lanterns and all. It seemed like he was doing all he could to attract the Apache."

Julep snorted. "I think you're giving Shinbone too much credit. I wouldn't say he's dumb, but he's not the sharpest knife in the kitchen."

And then, without a glance backward, the Indians blew out the lanterns, and prodded Julep, Slocum, and the fat man into a walk, their arms tied behind their backs, and they fell into line following the four horses. Broad Chest rode the lead horse, which happened to be Julep's. Slocum thought the choice showed that Broad Chest had decent taste in horseflesh. His own old mare, still looking mostly unperturbed, but tired, bore the sagged weight of the unconscious Shinbone.

"Why did Shinbone come back then, if he was planning on stealing from Deke?" said Julep. "He could have made a clean escape. It's not like Deke would ever go after him. He's so obsessed with his stockpile of weapons and with the Apache that he would just fume at Shinbone's absence, probably nothing more."

Mort looked shocked, as if he were just hearing something for the first time. "Why, Julep, I thought you would know."

Julep shook her head. "Know what?"

"Shinbone, he come back for you. Said you'd be waiting for him. Said he was going to take you away with him. He said he even got himself a piece of land back home and everything. Said you and him were going to start your own branch on the family tree."

While the fat man said this, Slocum watched Julep's face. It was all he could do to keep from laughing. The look of pure disgust that crept across her pretty features was a sight to behold. "Such a prospect can't be all that bad," said Slocum, trying to keep his face serious.

"Bad?" she said, loud enough that several of the Apache regarded her with their peculiar looks of contempt.

"Oh, I don't know. Shin's okay. You know how he can be, Julep. You'll have a fine family with him." Mort's eyes widened at the unspoken thought.

"Mort," Julep sighed. "Look around you."

Mort did as she bade him. The sullen, silent Apache men tromped alongside them, but a few feet away.

"You honestly think they're going to let us live?"

Mort's eyes widened and his jowly face shook in fear.

"Even if they did, Shinbone isn't likely to be in any sort of shape to go off on his own. Likely he'll end up fighting with or against Deke."

Mort swallowed. "Then you ain't sweet on Shin neither?"

Now it was Julep's turn to stifle a laugh. "Not hardly, Mort. He's my mother's brother."

"So?" Mort sounded to Slocum as if he were serious.

"Mort," said Julep, taking her time. "Shinbone is my uncle."

"Yeah, I know that. Heck, I'm your cousin and I been sweet on you since forever." The fat man smiled as he said it.

Slocum wondered just how it could be that the world had

gotten as populated as it had without more mishaps and madness. And then he thought about all those fools back East in cities and figured maybe he was wrong. Maybe it hadn't gotten all that far. Maybe the world would be filled with all manner of lots more impressive inventions and smarter people running around, if only . . .

The Apache were slowing their pace. Slocum looked up from his reverie. He had a plan; he just needed to figure out the best time to get it in motion. As plans went, it wasn't much of one, but it would have to do. Now all he had to do was worry about timing.

As they descended down a wide packed trail that narrowed as it snaked toward a jumble of boulders, he saw the one thing that could turn his plan from success to failure, or vice versa, in the blink of an eye. For there, standing proud and lean atop the rocks, with her hands on her hips, stood the little Apache princess who had been somewhat responsible for him finding himself in this mess.

As they passed by the rock, she stared down at them. Slocum caught her eye, but if she recognized him, she gave no indication. Though he did fancy that when her eyes fell on Julep beside him—tall, proud, blond, and white Julep—they narrowed. What might that mean? His entire plan hinged on whether the chief, the princess's father, would believe him about Deke's weapons stash and plans.

14

Deke had never been so angry in all his long days. And in the past few years he'd had a boatload of things to be angry about. He wanted to say that it had all started going to the dogs when that damned Slocum had flopped down from on high into their midst. But that wasn't really the case, and he knew it deep in his thumping rebel heart.

But he didn't really want to admit what he knew to be the dawning truth—he was being chewed apart from the inside of his family. For that was what he thought of the entire group of people he'd brought here to this magical canyon. He felt like their big daddy, their savior, and their leader, all rolled into one. He'd always been a big man, big as a bull grizz, as his friend and kinsman, Shinbone, used to say.

But that damned Shin, he'd been gone for too long now. Deke had foolishly thought that he could trust ol' Shin with more and more duties. He'd had bad luck lately with the younger men, all wanting more and more power, more excuses to up and leave the canyon, and what was it getting him?

That was why he'd begun to explain things to that Slocum, to show him the weapons cave, to introduce him to the boys, all the rest of them. That Slocum, Deke just knew he was a straight shooter. Or at least he'd thought he'd been. And now he up and absconded with Julep? His very own sister!

Deke looked around their own cave. They'd made it right nice. He always slept out on a pallet by the fire, which he felt was only right, given that Julep was his sister. He'd always felt bad that she never really seemed to settle on anyone. Lots of men here in the canyon would give their teeth (what ones they had left) to marry up with her, but she was a finicky sort.

And then, lo and behold, John Slocum drops out of the sky and he ends up being the man she sets her cap on. Deke just knew it, could tell by the way she started singing again around the fire, when she was cooking and when she was cleaning, gathering wood. Heck, she'd laid off complaining that there weren't enough women around to talk with.

Incredibly, she'd even stopped voicing her doubts about Deke's predictions that the Bluebellies were coming around looking for the Southern rebels. The holdouts, as Deke liked to think of himself and the rest of his brood. They were holding out, all right. But only long enough to stockpile arms, and recruit enough fighters to foul the North-led army's plans of broadening the great U.S. empire, even though they had all but crushed every last speck of happiness and humanity from good old Mother South.

"We'll see who leaves old Deke and gets away with it." He stared at the cold cook fire, at the neat row of Dutch ovens, lids and bales all lined up, scrubbed and seasoned, at the coffeepot resting on the rock, at the crock Julep kept all the spoons and knives standing in. She'd left it all as she did every day after the morning meal, as if she was coming back. But here it was early morning again, and she was still missing, along with that rascal, Slocum.

Only one of two explanations he could think of would account for this odd turn of events. Could be that Slocum had kidnapped Julep, and that one had to be the case. Because the other didn't bear thinking about. No way in hell could a good rebel gal like Julep abandon her family and willingly run off with Slocum. He'd said he was a Southerner, but he sure as hell didn't act like one. No, Deke was wrong about it all, had been, and that ate him up inside worse than rats gnawing on the dead at Shiloh.

And it stuck in his craw like a big old hunk of bad food that he couldn't bring himself to swallow. So Deke did the next best thing he could think of whenever he was faced with such a situation—the same thing he always did when he was angry and frustrated—he slipped into a blind burst of anger.

A film of gray-blue muck seemed to slide down over his eyes. He felt blood pump into his temples, and pulse there like tiny fists. He gritted his teeth and roared an unintelligible oath, then lashed out with a big ham of a leg, his boot clocking the nearest set of stacked pots.

The vessels scattered, bouncing off nearby rocks and the logs arranged for his people to sit at during meetings. Utensils sprayed across the dormant campfire, clattering over rocks. Still, he wasn't satisfied. Deke's big chest heaved with pent-up rage for all the wrongs he felt he'd experienced since long, long before the war, back when he was half the size he was now. Back when his pap would come lurching home, reeking of corn liquor, howling for blood because something around the little farm wasn't done right, some little thing had been forgotten.

Pap never seemed to remember that Deke might well have been big for his age—something that he always was his entire life—but he was still a boy and not able to run the whole place, the whole farm the way Pap wanted it run. As Deke grew older, he felt sure that if he could only talk with Pap, he could let him know he needed help. Maybe if Pap spent more time helping Deke and the other children tend to the place, to the livestock and the sorghum crop and the hay, instead of suckling on the mouth of that corn liquor jug every afternoon—and sometimes in the mornings, too— why, that might be just the thing to make the farm useful again. So one day he did just that.

Even as Deke lurched about the canyon camp, scattering the firewood stacks and ripping up the rock fire ring, stomping Julep's bedding, tossing her clothes and hurling everything about the once-neat place, he recalled that run-in with Pap with a clarity that he only ever experienced in his hate dreams, as he called them.

What he saw was Pap, big ol' Pap, bigger a man than even massive Deke would turn out to be, bent low over him, his broad black leather belt sliding out of his trouser loops as if it were a snake. And he remembered how Pap commenced to whomping on Deke as if he were putting out a fire.

All these slashing, spiky, searing memories came back to him as he lurched about the place that had been his home, the campsite he had shared with Julep. The one he'd always protected, the one who had warned him about so much. About Pap, about the war, about his dear dead wife, about storing all those weapons, all of it. She'd warned him about the canyon, said it would never be home, could never take the place of the dear old homeplace.

But he'd never listened, and now look at his life, look at this place. For months his people, his chosen family, had slowly been pulling away from him, pulling back from all the goodness he was sure to come, if only they would stay on track with him, believe in him. Wasn't he their savior, after all? Wasn't he their leader? Their father figure? Wasn't he their . . . pappy?

Long minutes after he had begun his rampage, Deke spun slowly to a standstill just before the spot where the campfire had, until a short time before, resided. Now it was a mere smear of blackened cinders. His massive chest rose and fell with his rapid breathing, his beard flecked with spittle and sweat. His hands hung at his sides, trickles of warm blood drip-drip-dripping from his fingertips.

The hollow wash of sound made by his pumping blood slowly receded, not unlike ocean waves pulled back before their next rush in. Deke heard a regular hugging, rasping sound, as if a locomotive were working its way hard up a steep grade, and not doing a very good job of making it to the top. He realized with a start that it was his own breathing. And it was matched in counterpoint by his hammering heart, doing its best to drive a hole through his chest wall.

On and on he huffed, and louder and louder his breathing grew until he finally felt like he was getting the better of it. Deke opened his eyes, and the world was fuzzy. He shook his head as if to dispel an annoying bee, and looked again. Gathered in a mass before him, huddled together, were most of his fellow canyon dwellers. They stood staring at him, cowering with their heads bowed, their shoulders slumped, their eyes cast upward in the middle as if drowning in a deep pool of fear. They even clutched at one another like children with their hands wrapped tight in their mamas' aprons.

He tried to speak, but could only manage a weak croak. He cleared his throat and tried again. "What do you all want?" he said. "Seems to me you could find a better way of going about your business than coming to watch me . . . rearrange my camp." But his normally jovial voice sounded blown out and raspy. "You hear?"

"Deke." A short, thin man stepped forward and held up his hands as if he expected he was about to be shot. "You got to go easy on us. Not too many of us here seen any men, 'specially you, act in such a manner. You was a wild man, Deke. We tried to stop you, but not a one of us could get near enough to you to do anything of use."

Deke looked around at the mess he'd made. He'd lived

in fear that this might happen again. It had been years since he'd done such a thing.

"Anybody hurt?" he said in a deep, raspy voice.

"Just you," said the thin man. "You're a bloodied mess, Deke. Wish you'd let one of us take a look at them hands of yourn."

Deke held up his hands before his face. The very act of raising them sent rockets of pain lancing up his sides, up his forearms, and through his shoulders. But that was nothing compared to the agonizing sight the bloodied, shredded fingertips brought to his still-clouded mind.

The gory spectacle transported him back to the battlefield, to the worst day of them all, when both sides, the Rebs and the Yanks, came at each other in a thrashing flurry of hellfire. The thunderous clapping of cannon fire resounded all about them; brutal fusillades slammed everything that dared move for what seemed like miles around. Horses screamed, still running the last few feet their big, proud bodies would ever run, unaware that one of their back legs had been punched clean off by a cannonball.

Bayoneted men lurched back and forth at each other; men tried to scream but blood gouting from their open mouths prevented it. And in the midst of it all, Big Deke, as he was known then, stumbled from Bluebelly to Bluebelly, stabbing and thrusting a saber he took off a dead colonel. He hacked at anything that looked remotely Northern, relishing every single stroke.

Deke took two bullets that day, one in the neck—it came out just under his chin, and gave him the reason to wear his full beard thereafter—and another in his meaty thigh. Neither wound slowed him in the least. If anything, they fired him up further. But this was the same way he'd been on every single battlefield, every single patrol at which they found Bluebellies encamped, every single time since the war ended that he found a carpetbagger who'd taken over a solid old Southern homestead for his own, had appropriated land that had once belonged to a fine Southern family.

It wouldn't take but a minute or two of conversation, a carefully worded question or two, for Deke to learn that the man and his foul wife and children were not from the Heart of Dixie. Something would happen, sometimes he could feel his men tugging on his arms in an effort to calm him, but it was no use. He would see that sticky gray-blue mass commence to wash over him, feel the blood pump and throb as if his forehead would burst apart. Sound would become a storm of clanking and thunder and the snap and crack of a wide black leather belt, falling hard and fast, over and over and over.

And now it had happened once more. He stared at his bloodied hands and felt odd, not like it was going to happen again, but as if he were sick, sort of an all-over-his-body throbbing ache. And then he felt the earth rush up fast to meet his face, felt a pain on the back of his head, and knew no more.

15

Slocum was tired. Dog-tired. And as they were herded into the Apache camp, he knew his day had only just begun. He tried to edge a bit in front of Julep, but she was having none of it. He had gotten close enough to her on the walk to whisper to her about the boot knife. He'd waited until they were a sufficient number of steps ahead of Mort, the fat man, because he didn't trust him. If he was dimwitted enough to think Shinbone was the next Moses, then he couldn't be trusted with any information, vital or not.

Now that they were in the camp, he would do his best to protect her from the open leers of the young braves and the angry stares of the women. He scanned their camp. There were a few mangy curs, walking as if they spent their lives under the switch, ribs looking as if they might punch out through their tight hides, teeth bared at anything that came near them.

A number of poorly built huts leaned in various directions, propped up by rocks and a few well-worn poles. Small campfires smoldered and smoked. Several deer hides had been stretched on racks, partially scraped clean, and a particularly hard-looking dog stood under one, bugged eyes scanning the crowd. He'd taken the opportunity, while attention had been diverted by the newcomers, to sneak in and mooch a gristly meal of dried hide and hair. Slocum was glad their arrival could provide the beast with a snack.

This was a rough lot. If this was the entire tribe, they numbered three, maybe four dozen in all, small whimpering children, naked and filthy, included. And yet above, surprisingly clean and with shining hair and a bold, defiant look in her eyes, stood the young princess, or so he called her, on the same rock. Her hands were folded across her ample breasts, her hide dress much cleaner than those on the other women.

What was her secret? And more to the point, where was her father, the chief? Slocum didn't see anybody who might resemble a chief. In full daylight, not even Broad Chest looked much like a chief, even though hours before, the big Indian had been only too willing to let Slocum assume that he was.

He looked up at the princess. It was as if she'd awaited his eye, and when she caught his gaze, she looked proudly up the rocky ravine. Slocum followed her gaze and saw what she was looking toward, that the path continued on, snaking between the grimy people and the hovels before him. He saw a fuller, thicker plume of new smoke rising up from a fire farther on. This rocky place, it seemed, contained further mysteries.

"Where are you all takin' us?" shouted Mort, staggering forward as one of the warriors kicked his backside. "I got to have a rest, I tell ya! I'm about done in!"

"Shut up, Mort," hissed Julep. "You ain't helping matters by yammering and complaining."

Slocum chose to ignore Mort's increasing level of whining. The fat man had been blubbering about poor Shinbone being mistreated, about how Lemuel had been a good man, and that Mort also wasn't up to the task of walking much farther that day, not without rest. Apparently Shinbone had worked him hard, in an effort to punish him for losing the pack animal on their return to the canyon. But if it was sympathy that Mort was looking for, he wasn't about to get any from Slocum.

Then the wailing began. It drowned out poor Mort's whining. And even before Slocum looked to see where the noise was coming from, he knew it was for the two dead Apache. The ones he and Julep had killed. If they got out of this alive, it would be a miracle. Why in God's name had he thought he could pull this off? If he had any sense at all, he would have up and ridden off without a look back at any of them, left Julep in the canyon—somehow she was one strong-willed woman, so that would have been a heck of a trick—and headed any direction but toward the Apache camp.

Curse me for a fool, thought Slocum. But he knew he couldn't have gone in any other direction but toward the people who needed help. The Apache, no matter that they drove him to the brink, literally, nonetheless needed to know what was coming. And since he had few other options at present, he had to concentrate on convincing them that they were soon to be attacked. And unless they had some secret horde of warriors and weapons, they were doomed.

He had to convince them that they must flee this place. He believed they could outrun Deke's army, if only because they had no heavy weapons to lug with them. That argument, if he lived long enough to present it, would be tricky. The Apache were a proud, noble people who would likely consider fleeing to be on par with the lowest lows of cowardice. And that was something he could understand. But he had to convince them that leaving in this instance meant living to fight another day.

He also had to save his skin, Julep's skin, and though it

pissed him off, he supposed he was also responsible for the lives of Mort and Shinbone, too.

They were herded along the winding path, and while the wailing continued behind them, a few members of the gathered bedraggled Indians peeled off and joined the procession. Slocum assumed they were also mourning members of the dead Indians' close families. A cold knot of shame coiled in his gut, and anger with himself crept into his mind, though he had been forced into the killings.

"John." Julep looked at him, and he saw genuine fear in her eyes and a tear forming. "John, what can I expect from them? I mean to say . . . what will they do to me?" She straightened, thrust her chin out, and kept walking. "I want to be prepared," she said.

"You're a bold woman, Julep. Apache value that. Don't be anything less than what you are. But at the same time, try not to antagonize them. Mort keeps on running his mouth and he'll feel their sting."

As if he had been heard by the Apache nearest them, the man edged between them with a lance, as if to pry them apart.

"What are you doing?" said Julep.

Slocum said, "Remember what I said, Julep. Be strong, but don't antagonize. Don't be afraid to shout for me. I'll do my best to help you."

She nodded at him as they were led apart.

"Do not worry, white man," said a bold voice. Slocum looked from Julep to the man who had spoken. The man looked familiar, and Slocum knew he had to be the chief. He recognized him from the chase that day weeks before, as the man who had led the others on horseback and raged at him while they galloped hard on his heels across the flats.

"We are not animals. We do not kill needlessly, nor do we torture without cause. Unlike whites."

The man spoke very good English, and this told Slocum that he had most likely been educated in a white school, maybe by missionaries. But that line of questioning would have to wait.

Slocum watched as they led Julep to a small hut, hide-wrapped and low. One brave led her in and returned shortly. Slocum presumed they had tied her to something inside. He hoped so, as his mind raced through any number of other possibilities, none of which bore consideration.

He stopped struggling against his bonds and fixed the chief with a hard glare. "You had better hope so, Chief. I am not in a position to do much more than talk, I realize that, but I will promise you, if she is harmed in any way, and I have even the slightest opportunity to exact revenge, believe me, I will."

"I will keep that in mind, white man. And I will also make sure we don't give you that opportunity." The man seemed to almost smile, then he jerked his head to the side, nodded toward a hut similar to the one they'd stashed Julep in. Broad Chest prodded Slocum in the back, gestured toward the hut with his expressionless face.

"Hold on a minute. I have to talk with the chief."

The chief yammered in Apache tongue at the man, his eyebrows raised in question. Finally the chief nodded and stared at Slocum. "Talk now."

"You have got to get on out of here. This place is a powder keg waiting to be touched off."

The chief actually looked as though he might smile. "What makes a white man say such things? Always it is something terrible that the Apache must do, all for the sake of the white man."

"I understand how you might feel that way, but you have to listen to me. It's about those folks down in the canyon. I know all about it and how it used to be your home."

"You are from there."

"Not exactly. I spent time there, but I sort of . . . dropped in on them. While I was there, I found out that they have a whole lot of weapons stockpiled down there—and you and your people are their first target. Any day now."

The chief regarded him for a long moment, then said, "Did you kill my people?"

Slocum felt that the chief already knew the answer, but as he opened his mouth to respond, a howl of rage from behind him made him turn.

There was Shinbone, weaving and unsteady, his shirt ripped off his back and hanging in shreds, and a crazed look in his glassy eyes. He held a gleaming knife, the cutting edge of the blade held tight against the fleshy roll of Mort's neck. The fat man gasped, his mouth working like that of a beached fish, his dimpled hands pawing at Shinbone's sinewy forearms, wrapped tight across Mort's flabby chest.

"Stay back, you savage bastards!" Shinbone spun Mort this way and that as the Apache, all grinning—obviously enjoying this rare spectacle—gathered into an ever-tightening ring around him.

Slocum guessed that when the Apache cut his straps that bound his wrists to his ankles and let him flop off the horse, they might have cut too much. Shinbone, probably playing possum, had bided his time and took the chance as it presented itself.

"Shin," gagged Mort. "What you doing? Gaah! Shin?"

"Shut up, damn your worthless hide. You're my ticket out of this viper nest. You open your mouth one more time and I'll carve that flapping tongue out for once and all."

It seemed to Slocum as if Shinbone was regaining his balance and vision more and more by the second. The Apache didn't appear to be in any hurry to prod ol' Shin; rather it looked as if they were enjoying themselves. And then the unexpected happened. A young Apache burst through the line just behind Shinbone. He was muscled out well, and nearly as tall as a full-grown man. Despite all that, Slocum didn't think he was much more than fourteen years old, and reminded Slocum of the youth they'd had to kill back at the canyon's mouth.

But what caught everyone's attention was the knife he wielded. Unlike Shinbone's, this one did not glint in the sunlight, but looked to be a dark, vicious slab of well-used, well-bloodied metal. As Shinbone turned, lugging struggling Mort by the neck, with no hesitation the young warrior thrust the dagger halfway up Shinbone's back, just to the side of his spine.

The tall man's eyes snapped impossibly wide, his head jerked back on a stalk of veined neck that tightened and trembled. All the people gathered about him stared in quiet shock at what they had just seen. A thin stream of blood trickled from Shin's mouth, pushed out by an equally thin cry, as if made by a baby heard from far-off. Then the tall man's body convulsed, and as he did so, the knife he held to Mort's fat neck sank in deep.

Mort's eyes grew rounder, even as blood welled over the blade, slowly spilling down his shirtfront. The wound—and Shinbone's tight grip—prevented Mort from screaming, though his mouth pantomimed it well. But Mort's feeble pawing grip seemed to grow stronger as Shinbone's waned. The fat man swung and bucked and spun, and somehow this burst of power forced the spinning, bleeding mass of two men to spin, in an odd death dance, while those around them merely watched in horror at the quick-fire scene. The Indian boy, still holding the handle of his knife, worked it deeper into Shin's back, a determined look on the youth's face, his teeth gritted, and his eyes squinting at the blood beginning to spray at him. Only then did the boy release his hold on the deep-set knife.

A last burst of reflexive energy from Shinbone whipped the tall man's knife arm outward in a wide arc. As he spun, the blood-drenched tip of the long blade caught the youth square in the chest and lodged there.

All three stabbed figures stood erect, eyes wide, staring

at everyone, staring at nothing, at the last things they each would ever see, perhaps the clear blue sky, a high-up cloud scudding slowly from somewhere to somewhere, before the beauty of the world winked out for each of the three dead men, and they collapsed in a lifeless pile of meat.

Slocum had never seen anything quite like that before. Apparently neither had anyone else. For what seemed an eternal minute, the gathered Apache stared in disbelief at the instant horror they had witnessed. All told, the gruesome event had taken no more than a few quick seconds, perhaps the time it takes to shout to a friend.

And then the wailing really started. The only thing Slocum could be grateful for was that Julep hadn't had to see it. No matter what type of men Shinbone and Mort had been, they were still her kin, if not her friends. It was bound to be a shock when she found out what had happened.

One howling voice rose above the rest, a reedy, tremulous thing that rang with the grief of a long life lived in a hard way. Slocum traced it to a thin old man who pushed his way through the crowd and hunched over the young dead man. He pushed at the bodies of Mort and Shinbone until some of the other warriors grasped the dead white men and dragged them off the body of the youth. The old man bent low over the boy's body, wailing and beating his fists against the boy's stilled chest.

Finally he ceased, but his eyes, rimmed with red and set above a long, hawklike nose and grim slit of a mouth, seemed to search the crowd until they settled on Slocum. With speed that betrayed his apparent age, the old man leapt to his feet and let the young man's head drop unceremoniously to the bloodied earth. He screeched something in Apache, but Slocum didn't need to know the lingo to gather that the old man didn't want to palaver over a cup of hot coffee.

"Chief, what's he want?" Slocum asked without taking his eyes from the advancing old man.

"That boy was his grandson. He loved him very much. The old one wants blood coup."

"But I didn't kill the kid." Slocum braced for the old man's attack. Rarely had Slocum seen anyone so determined.

"That doesn't matter. To him, you are white, and that is enough to fight for."

"I'd rather we spent the time discussing what I came here to tell you—that the whites in the canyon are planning on attacking you all."

But by then the old man had stalked up to Slocum and begun ranting in his face. Spittle flecked from his mouth. Unlike Shinbone's final moments, when everyone saw his stumpy black teeth gnashing the air as if he were chewing a troublesome wad of gristle, the old man's teeth were impressive, white, and whole. And up close, he looked a whole lot younger. His body was leaner, less wrinkled, and more muscled than Slocum had first seen. Perhaps the shock of seeing his grandson die was too brutal for him and so at first he had seemed frailer.

The old man wasn't concerned with politeness and stepped in close, thrusting his hands, palms out, into Slocum's chest. He kept at it, no one interfering, pushing Slocum backward, though Slocum was having as little of it as he could stand, and tried to push back with his head and chest. He didn't want to harm the old man, but he was being urged to fight.

"I'm not the man who killed your grandson!" he shouted, even though he knew, according to the chief, that the old man didn't care. He just wanted blood revenge on a white. And he was the only white around—except Julep. That thought changed everything.

Finally, Slocum held his ground, a difficult thing to do with the old man coming at him like a determined lynx. "Enough!" shouted Slocum. To the chief, he said, "I will fight him, but he is old, and it will not be a fair fight. Just please don't let him take it out on the white woman. She had nothing to do with any of this. She is innocent. As innocent as are you and most of your people. Do you hear me?"

The chief clapped his hands above the hubbub and noise of the crowd. A number of warriors, some of whom Slocum recognized, gathered around in another ragged circle. One man slit the ropes binding Slocum's wrists, and he muttered a low groan of relief, rubbing his raw wrists tenderly.

The chief tossed two knives to the dirt between Slocum and the old man and nodded toward them, muttering something. To Slocum, he merely said, "Only one lives."

The old man, once again showing his catlike agility, snatched up a knife, then retreated a few paces, allowing Slocum to do the same. Once each man was armed, they circled like game cocks in a ring, the old man nearly smiling, his sneer was so wide.

He growled and lunged, closing the gap between them. Slocum sidestepped, but at the last second, the old man's knife flicked and caught Slocum in the side, slicing through his shirt and nicking his rib cage. It stung and served to remind Slocum that the old man was indeed out for his blood, every last drop of it, if his determined look was any indication.

They continued in such a fashion, with the gathered crowd beginning to enjoy the blood sport. The chanting increased, and the crowd pressed closer. Sweat stung Slocum's eyes, and he learned quickly that the old man was more than his match. It could well prove to be Slocum's last go-round. But not without a damn good fight, he told himself, and in a move that broke the little dancing routine the two combatants had locked themselves into, Slocum spun in the opposite direction and drove a dusty boot into the side of the old man's head.

The leathery face snapped sideways, a tooth pinged from the angry mouth like a thrown pebble, and the old man's shoulders sagged. But only for a moment. Then he recovered, danced back in, closer than Slocum had expected. The old man lunged in tight once more, hoping to catch Slocum with an upper-thrusting blow to the gut. But Slocum had been in his share of fights, enough to know what to expect from such a move. He parried again, and as the old man overshot, Slocum spun to the side, then quickly drove the butt end of the knife's thick handle down hard at the base of the old man's skull. The old Apache dropped to the dusty earth like a sack of rocks.

Not quite unconscious, the old man lolled facedown in the dirt in a daze. Slocum staggered over and kicked the knife from the gnarled hand, then looked briefly at the weapon in his own hand before tossing it beside the other one, at the feet of the chief.

"Only one lives," said the chief, a dour look on his dark face.

"Nothing doing." Slocum shook his head, trying to catch his breath. "The old man's angry, but he's angry with the boy, not with me. The boy brought his death on himself." He jerked a thumb at his chest. "I had nothing to do with it." He held his arms wide and walked slowly around the circle, staring into the faces that stared back at him. "I came here to warn you about the white men who would do you much harm. I didn't have to do that, you know. Why do you suppose I did that?" He paused before the chief. "Now will you listen to me?"

The chief stared at him a moment, then cut his eyes to the old man, whose labored breathing had begun to soften and even out. To Broad Chest, he said, "Help the old one to care for his grandson." He looked back to Slocum, but still addressed Broad Chest. "And tie this one to the post in the hut."

As he was led away, his wrists cinched tighter than ever, Slocum said, "So that's it, eh? You're a fool, Chief. A prideful fool." Slocum knew that uttering such words to an Apache chief could well get him killed. And he didn't care. What more could they do but kill him? "Damn fools," he muttered as he sagged, exhausted, against the pole in the middle of a dark, dank hut.

16

He awoke in the dark to the sound of soft feet padding their way into the dark little skin-covered hut. Someone had entered and was drawing close. He tensed his muscles, though there was little else he could do, considering his wrists and feet were bound to the pole. He felt sure that if he worked it hard enough, he could probably pull out the pole, but all that would do was collapse the structure and leave him under it. What good would that do? No, he had to try to get at that boot knife. He could still feel it was there.

"Slocum? John Slocum?" It was the Indian girl. He didn't think she was any more pleased to see him than her tribesmen had been, but he somehow didn't think she had it in her to kill him. But then again, after today's events, what did he know?

A cool hand touched his forehead, slipped down his face. "Are you hurt, John Slocum?"

"Hello, Princess," he whispered, matching her own lowered tone of voice. "Well, I've been more comfortable, I can tell you that much."

He felt her warm breath, smelled its musky, honeyed

scent as she breathed close to his cheek. "Maybe I can help," she said.

"Please, yes. Cut these bindings. I can barely feel my hands and feet."

"They tied your feet, too?"

"Mm-hmm. Hey, what are you doing?" He felt her fingers snaking into his boot, then a slight chuckle, and she withdrew his boot knife. "How did you know about that?"

"A long time ago, I watched you dress, remember?"

"Hmm."

She slipped the blade through the hide wraps around his ankles and his feet were freed. The relief was instant, and Slocum spread his legs cautiously, easing his boots back and forth, flexing his feet and calves. The pain would come soon, pins and needles like fire ants crawling up his legs. But he could sustain them. He'd been in similar situations before and he knew that the pain meant he still had limbs that would work.

"Okay, now my wrists."

But she tensed.

"What's wrong?"

"I thought I heard something," she said in a quieter whisper.

"I think it was my heart," he said, half joking.

"No, no."

"Princess, cut my wrists free, dammit."

"That's no way to talk, John Slocum. I only want to help you."

He felt her pull away, as if she might leave.

"I know, Princess. Just cut me loose and I'll be glad to thank you properly."

"What do you have in mind, John Slocum?" But she only teased him by whispering close to his face again. He felt her warm breath on his cheek, fluttering his eyelashes.

Then her hands were working his belt, then the buttons on the fly of his denims. "Princess, what are you doing?"

He felt her hand slide into his parted trousers, felt the warmth of her slim fingers as they closed around his member, already nearly full with an uncontrollable urge.

"I am doing just what you want me to, I believe."

He swore he could see her smiling in the dark.

She was standing before him, but now she slowly knelt. Again, he felt her hot breath on him, but much lower down now. And soon her warm mouth touched him at the tip, kissed him tenderly there, as if it were a special flower that required such a reaction. She did an odd thing then. She rubbed it against her cheek, under her nose, across her mouth, to the other side of her face, as if she were marking herself with his scent. It was odd, but it felt so good to him. Even in his current situation, it provided a much-needed distraction from the uncertainty of his predicament. He vaguely wondered if Julep was being well treated. He hoped not as well treated as he was . . .

"Oh, John Slocum," the Indian maiden murmured, then whispered a flurry of quiet, hurried oaths in Apache, before taking him fully into her mouth. He felt himself bumping the back of her throat, and still it seemed she wanted more. He heard her breathe through her nostrils, matching her increasing rhythm with her breathing, her tongue snaking under his shaft with strength, drawing back on him lightly with her teeth.

She pulled on him as if she were sipping water from a stream, pulling, pulling, harder and faster with each backward motion of her head. He wanted to hold her hair, guide her to a slower rhythm, savor the moments there in the dark with this Indian princess.

Before he realized it, he felt himself tighten, felt sure she was going to drain him any second, but with a smacking sound, she stopped.

She, too, had sensed the coming explosion and wished to avoid it, he guessed. Or perhaps she wished to prolong it. Fine with him, as long as she didn't just leave. The thought made him momentarily tense. Until he felt her breath on his face again. She was pressing into him now, very close, and he couldn't even reach out and knead the twin mounds of her backside. What he really wanted to do was part them and . . .

She had the same idea. He heard the lower part of her deer hide dress slide up, just enough, he bet, and then her heat warmed the tip of him once again. He felt her hands spreading herself wide over him, and then she was on him, and slid down over him slowly, fully, until he filled her tightness.

Her breath leaked out in a stuttering whisper, and she stayed like that as deep as she could take him, as if she were savoring a toothsome treat. Then he felt her hands on his shoulders and she lifted herself up just a bit. One leg rose up, then the other. With her legs wrapped around him, she began pulling away, then toward him, over and over, faster and faster, until her breathing once again came at a rapid rate, matching her fevered efforts. He did his best to buck with her, in counterpoint to her hard-driving rhythm. Her mouth and nose were pressed to his neck, and soon he felt her bite him lightly, as if to keep from screaming.

Then he felt the reason why—she pulled back once, twice, then hung there, squeezing him hard, milking him with an unseen hand.

"Oh, John Slocum," she said in a slow, weary sigh.

They stayed that way for the better part of a minute, until she parted from him and rebuttoned his denims. Then she stood before him in the dark.

"Thank you, John Slocum. That was the only nice thing to happen to me here in this foul place."

"Why do your people live here?" he said. "Surely there are other Apache you could join up with."

Princess said, "My people are what you would call outcasts."

"What did they do to earn that word?"

"A long time ago they refused to do something, that is more to the point."

Slocum didn't ask what she meant, hoped instead she'd offer the information. But after a few seconds, it was clear she wasn't about to tell him, so he changed the subject. "Do you know what the chief plans to do?"

She didn't look at him.

Finally he said, "Princess, please. I have to know. Every second he waits is another second that Deke and his people gain on you. We cannot let that happen."

She spun fast on him, fire blazing in her dark eyes. "Why do you care? Why do you care what happens to my people?"

"If you put it that way, I don't care what happens to your people."

Her smug smile dropped as he continued to speak.

"Any more than I care what happens to any other people I come across in my travels. But it's different when someone, hell anyone, has a rough run of it, and especially if they're treated poorly by others who have no right to treat them that way."

"I don't understand what you mean."

Slocum squinted in the dank little hut, thought about a better way to explain himself, but before he could reply, the chief's voice cut in. "This white man would have us believe that we should have our sacred dwelling place back."

The well-muscled older man pushed the rest of the way in from the doorway. "He says that what the white devils have done to us has been wrong, that he can somehow save us from their guns. He says many things, but always out of one side of his face. The other lies even to himself."

Slocum shifted on the pole, wincing at the cutting pain in his wrists as the leather dug in deeper. There was no comfortable position when you were tied tight to a pole by the wrists. It felt as though the bindings were made of hot wire dipped in liquid fire. He supposed he should be grateful that they weren't also lashed around his forehead.

"Whatever happened to hospitality?" he asked aloud.

Neither the chief nor the princess responded, but Slocum could tell she was bothered by seeing him in pain like this, and he was glad for it. Maybe it would convince her that he spoke the truth. After all, what could he possibly have to gain by lying to her? This last thought emboldened him enough that he gave voice to it.

"How could I possibly benefit from having come back to you now? As you can see, I'm not in the best of shape, you have my horse, most of my gear. As much as I like my old Appaloosa and my own bedroll and such, they aren't worth risking my neck, or the neck of the woman who is with me. We could have gladly gone on our way, keeping our distance from you. But that didn't happen, did it?"

"He speaks the truth," said the princess.

"He makes me angry," said the chief in a low growl, not taking his gloomy, heavy-lidded eyes from Slocum.

"Leave. Now." The chief said this to the young woman. She regarded him haughtily for a moment, then obeyed. The chief glowered for another few seconds, then he, too, turned to go.

"Chief!" barked Slocum, his voice carrying as much anger as had the Apache leader's. It was forceful enough to stop the man in his tracks, though the chief didn't turn around.

"Dammit, man, you have to listen to me. That canyon is filled with angry whites, more than you have here, and there are more on the way. They'll be here any day now. But the worst of it is they have enough firepower—guns, ammunition, cannons, Gatling guns, explosives, you name it, they have it—to kill every single one of you, your family, all the women, children, the old, the sick, it won't matter."

The chief didn't move, so Slocum continued. "Those

white men in the canyon are angry, not just at you, but at a whole lot of other people, too. But you and your people will be the first to die. All your warriors on horseback with arrows and spears and war clubs and axes, they won't make a bit of difference against all those white man's guns. And the sad thing about all this is . . . you know it. You know that what I'm saying is the truth."

To Slocum's surprise, the chief let the deer hide door flap slip closed. He turned once again to face Slocum. This time, though, he looked as if he'd aged ten years in two minutes. His once-rigid shoulders sagged, his wide, bright eyes looked dimmed, even in the darkened interior of the hut, and his firm-set jaw had dropped as the man bent his head, considering all that Slocum had told him.

"Chief," Slocum said in a quieter voice. "Unless you do something soon, your people will die."

"There is nothing that can be done. We cannot leave this place. As bad as it is, this is our home now. And one day, perhaps our sacred canyon will once again become our home."

He looked up at Slocum, who saw for the first time the weight of leadership on this man's shoulders. He was looking at a tired, broken man. "Chief, it will take much more than hope. And it will take more effort than you have given, more planning, more of everything, most of these things you do not have. And the more sickness your people experience, the weaker your tribe becomes."

"You think I do not know this? You speak to me as if you know of hardship. We are outcasts. This small band of Apache, we are all that remain of a group that left others, a warring tribe." He almost growled the words, turning away.

Then he spun back and said, "When my father's fathers found the canyon, they knew it was a gift from the Great Spirit Father, a gift that we must treat with respect. My people long ago settled here, for it was a land of plenty." He gestured wide with both hands to indicate the unforgiving landscape beyond the dim walls of the hut.

"And all was well for a long time. No one bothered us, we lived in peace, the whites traveling were unaware of us, even as they sought ways to venture down into our little world. But we all knew that it could not last forever. That one day the whites, for there were so many of them, would find us."

As he spoke, he walked behind Slocum. He waited for the chief to free his wrists, but the man, smiling, walked back around to face Slocum.

As if reading his mind, the chief said, "Not yet. You have not proven to me I can trust you."

Slocum nodded. "Fair enough. But let me ask you—how did you and your people learn to speak such good English if you spent so much time isolated down in the canyon?"

Again, the chief's sly smile stretched across his face. It made him look younger, more confident. "I never said that the foul whites who now reside in our canyon were the first to come among us."

"There were others?" Slocum had assumed Deke and his cohorts were the first.

"There was one other. An old white woman. We do not know how, but she had been traveling with a burro, carrying books, walking alone across this land." He shook his head at the memory.

"This was a long time ago. I was but a young man then. She made her way down among us. We were afraid, but when we found that she was alone, and that she wished us no harm, we slowly welcomed her into our lives. She stayed with us for a long time, and taught us many things, as we did for her. She learned the Apache tongue and we learned her English. We also learned to read her books. She taught one of us, then more and more, until many of us took up these new ways."

"What happened to her?" asked Slocum.

"Time took her, as it will all of us. But she was an old, old thing by then. She had become more one of us than we had become white."

"Was she . . . among those in the burial ground at the far end of the canyon?"

The chief nodded. "Yes," he said. "the place the whites have desecrated. I do not know if good can ever be brought back there."

"First you need to be alive to be able to try, don't you think?"

The chief regarded him a moment. "You do not lie about this, do you?"

"No, Chief, I am not lying."

"I believe you," said the chief, and once more turned to go.

"Then why don't you do something about it? Why don't you at least let me go?"

"There is one simple reason." He looked back at Slocum. "The girl."

"The girl?" Slocum felt a knot tighten in his gut. "You mean your daughter?"

The chief smiled, shook his head as if pitying Slocum. "She is not my daughter. She is my wife."

17

Deke watched approvingly as the dozens of fresh-faced new recruits lined up for inspection. They'd streamed down into the canyon's southern—and only—entrance late the day before, in good spirits and ready to begin what Deke had told Shinbone and the others who were out recruiting for the cause was going to be a hell of a second coming. The "Second Rising of the South" was what Deke had actually taken to calling it.

Cooter, the man he'd selected to be a sort of second in command under Shinbone, told him that old Shin had taken Lemuel and Mort and split off from the main group of recruiters. Said they had to go on a secret, special mission for Deke, but that they'd meet them back at the canyon. Coot was surprised that Shin and the boys hadn't been there when he'd arrived with all the recruits and the wagons of fresh supplies. They'd even managed a few more cases of weapons and ammunition, which they'd left up top, under guard. Said they'd also found some blood near the canyon entrance. Looked to be a scuffle of sorts had taken place.

All this news—the odd little revolt of Rufus and kin, the

disappearance of Julep and Slocum, Shinbone's "secret mission" that Deke had no knowledge of, and then Shin and the boys' disappearance—why, it made Deke's head swim. What could it all possibly mean?

He had spent a good hour roving back and forth in the rubble of his wrecked campsite, massaging his bandaged hands. It dawned on him later, hours after he'd trashed the place, that it was as it should be. It was a sign from God telling him to leave the canyon forever, take the arms, lead his people in a mighty uprising against the foul Bluebellies.

And today was the day. He'd see what they were made of, first hauling up all the weapons from the secret cave guarded by his own sons, then they'd cut their teeth in battle against the filthy savage Apaches. Them dropping the rock on Henry's head let Deke know that they were still around, still playing their Indian games.

And now here he was, inspecting the troops, his troops, and truth be told, he'd seen better. They were a ramshackle lot, straw hats, bare feet, no shirts, lots of corncob pipes, barely a few dozen teeth between the lot of them . . . But he wasn't about to tell them what disappointments he saw. After all, these people were Southern folk, and when the true test came, as he suspected it would, by gum, they'd show their true worth.

"Now you all have listened to me yammer on for pretty near an hour. And you're all still here, so I guess that means y'all wanna stick with me." He eyed them, noticed a few shocked looks, and realized that of course they planned on following him—they'd come all that way, hadn't they? On nothing more or less than the promise of seeing the South rise again.

Deke cleared his throat and said, "What I mean is . . . it's time to clear out the stockpile. I've had wagons brought over to the cave, and men have been working on loading her up. So you all head on over there and finish off helping, then we'll get them wagons on up to the top. You'll note that them wagons is narrow. That's to get them through those tight spots on the trail heading up to the rim. Now." He clapped his big hands together and winced at the pain his damaged fingers felt. "Any questions?"

A thin-as-a-reed fellow wagged a big-knuckled hand, then let it drop, as if holding it up was just too dang much work. He ran a few grimy fingertips along the stubble on his chin. "I reckon I could use a biscuit afore I set to work."

Deke stared at the man. He'd counted on Julep fixing food for them. Now she was gone, Lord knew where. Deke decided to take a hard approach. He rested his big ham hands on his hips and said, "You all get to work! I'll roust up some vittles for the road. We ain't got time to waste. Got to catch them Apaches while they're still denned up like the snakes they are!"

The crowd dispersed slowly. He heard that same man mutter something about biscuits. Deke was about to shout something at the man when another man came up to him, shorter but just as haggard looking, and said, "Don't see why we got to fight Apaches. I come here to get even with the damn North. Cooter said I'd get to kill me a pile of genuine U.S. Army Bluebellies and get rich in the process. Is that the way she's gonna run, Cap'n?"

Deke wanted to clout the man for questioning his plans, but he liked that the man called him "Cap'n," so he let it slide this time. "Yeah, it's gonna play out just like that. But we got to get them guns up top, or else we're sunk before we float. Got to deal with the Apaches as a sort of test, make sure the weapons run smooth. Then we head on over to the rail line. U.S. Army runs troops through there all the time, so that's where we'll start."

The man looked convinced, pooched out his lower lip, and nodded. "Sounds good to this ol' bird dog." He turned to go, but Deke stopped him.

"Hey, Bird Dog, you know what a Gatlin' gun is?"

The thin man rubbed his chin. "Seen one once."

"You like to run one?"

For the first time, the man's eyes widened. "You mean it?"

Deke nodded, smiling.

"Got me a chance to mow down a pile of Blues all at once." Bird Dog smacked his callused hands together and grinned. "Yee-haw!"

Deke watched him walk toward the arms cave with the others. For the first time in a couple of days, he felt like he had before Julep left. Once again he felt like maybe his plans were all going to work out. The Second Rising of the South!

18

Slocum couldn't believe everything he'd been hearing and seeing in the Apache camp. They truly didn't give a damn what happened. Maybe they were tired of running, of being driven out of their homes. But what was the chief thinking? From what Slocum saw, they had very few firearms, and the weapons they did have—bows and arrows, hand axes, and knives—would be less than useless against Gatling guns, rifles, cannons, revolvers, you name it.

And the princess was actually the chief's wife? No wonder he was pissed off. Slocum gritted his teeth and struggled again against the hide thongs, but between sweat and the swelling in his wrists, the more he struggled, the tighter they grew. Even if he could loosen them enough, he could barely reach his boots. He'd been seated against the base of the pole for hours since the chief left him. But he hadn't been idle.

He had used his numb fingers to dig at the hard-packed earth, trying to find the bottom of the pole. He felt sure that he'd succeeded in at least loosening the pole. With any luck he'd be able to stand soon and lift the thing out of the hole, then squat back down and somehow get his strapped hands out from under the pole. That was his paltry plan anyway.

Slocum smirked as sweat dripped off his nose. If the damned Apache wouldn't listen to reason, then at least he had to get Julep out of there. If she was still . . . No, he couldn't let himself think that way. She had to be alive. And he'd find her, steal a few horses, and head out as fast as those beasts could carry them. Get Julep away before her crazy brother and his rebel army came calling.

He paused and looked toward the door of the hut. He could see its faint outline, and he couldn't make it out but a short time before. That meant dawn was coming in another hour or so. He had to get out of there.

And then he heard a sound, a padding of feet outside. It was a sound he'd become familiar with. Couldn't mean Princess was back for more, could it? He didn't have the strength for more of her games. But he'd certainly try. He peered in the dark at the door and suddenly saw a shape emerge. Yep, looked like her, all right.

"John Slocum!" she whispered.

"I'm still here, Princess."

"Good. I will free you now."

Slocum sighed. "Good—but couldn't you have decided that a few hours ago?"

"Why? I thought you would be happy."

"I am, I am. It's just that I spent the last few hours—never mind. I'll need two horses. Where are they kept?"

"Two? But you are only one man," she said, pausing behind him.

He felt the cold steel of the blade of what was likely his boot knife against his wrist. "The other's for Julep. I have to get her out of here, too." He felt the blade slide away from the leather thongs. "What are you doing? Cut me loose, Princess."

"No, I cannot. Not if you are taking that woman, too."

"Why? Are you jealous?" Slocum half smiled in the dark.

"Yes. You take me with you instead. She is nothing. She is . . . a white."

"So am I," he said. She didn't reply, so he said, "Okay, okay. Have it your way. But untie me now, please."

She wasted no time in slicing through the tough leather, and he rolled forward, away from her, lest it be another strange Apache trick. He stood, a bit wobbly, and rubbed circulation back into his throbbing hands, then stomped in place.

"Now," he said in a whisper as she came close to him. "Which way to the horses?"

She turned slightly and pointed toward the mouth of the canyon. "They are kept beyond there. You passed the place on the way in. They graze during the day in a valley close by."

While she was still turned away from him, he muttered, "I'm sorry," then quick as an eye blink, he gave her a short, sharp jab to the temple, wincing inside even as he knew he was doing it in an effort to save them all. He caught her thin, limp form and carried her to the base of the pole, which he leaned her against. He tied her wrists loosely, just tight enough that she would have to work for a minute or so at undoing the knots. Then he groped the ground where she'd fallen and found his boot knife.

"Now, to Julep and the horses. And then we have to try to stop a one-sided range war."

He poked his head out of the hut, scanned the graying gloom of the silent camp. His presence would likely be detected by the camp dogs, but that was a chance he'd have to take. He made it to the hut where Julep had been taken, and hoped there wasn't anyone in there except her.

"Julep?" he whispered. No reply. He tried again, a little louder, but to no avail. It was possible he had the wrong shelter. He was about to leave and try another hut when he heard a small rustling sound. "Julep? That you?"

"John?" she whispered. "Is it . . . is it you, John?"

He headed toward the voice, found her tied as he'd been

to the center pole, and with his knife, cut her wrists and ankle bonds free. "Let's go," he said, rubbing her legs quickly. "Not much time."

He clamped a big hand around one of her wrists, and tugging her into a painful lope, they made their way through the camp toward the mouth of the little rocky canyon. As he guessed, a couple of dogs gave halfhearted growls and low yips, but they were likely too fatigued by hunger to do much more than that. He hoped so, because the last thing they needed was to be chased by curs.

They made their way to where he suspected the horses were kept and found them loosely corralled in a rocky pen. The early morning offered just enough light for him to see the horses, and make out the good from the bad. There among them, looking thin but otherwise in decent shape, stood his Appaloosa. "Hey, boy, hey, hey, remember me?"

Slocum searched the rails and there, cleaned and perched in the center, sat his own gear, the very gear he'd lost before he tumbled into the canyon. And piled on top of his saddle sat his coiled gun belt and Colt Navy revolver. Princess must have brought it all, anticipating riding off with him.

It took but a moment's work to saddle the Appaloosa, then he found another saddle and gear and did the same with a solid horse for Julep. The old mare that had carried him up and out of the canyon was there, standing hipshot and seemingly contented, as if this sort of thing happened to her all the time. He scratched her on the head, then on a whim, he left the corral poles down when he and Julep mounted up. The other four or five horses wouldn't go far, but maybe they could get in some grazing in the threadbare country nearby. It might also slow the Apache in following them.

Once they had put a mile between them and the Apache camp, Slocum said, "Did they mistreat you, Julep?"

She took a moment to answer, then said, "No. Not at all.

They even brought me food and water, two things they don't have much of. I see now that they're not what I thought, John. I was poisoned by Deke's hatred of them. Yes, they killed his wife, but they were only protecting their very way of life, a way of living that we stole from them. I see it all now, John."

"Good, then I hope you'll help me head back to the canyon and try to convince Deke not to do this crazy thing."

"Of course. But we'd better hurry."

"Why, do you know something I don't?"

She shook her head as she nudged the horse to go faster. "No," she shouted, "but I know he was planning on doing something as soon as the new recruits returned—and they're overdue."

"But I thought Shinbone and his cohorts were the only ones to return."

"No, no, no." She shook her head. "Cooter was his deputy, and he's never let Deke down yet. He'll have brought back plenty of folks with him."

"Well, that's just dandy," said Slocum, heeling the Appaloosa into an all-out run, wondering who in the hell Cooter was . . .

Sometime later, in the clear morning light, they saw the very thing they didn't want to see: a cloud of dust boiling toward them from a half mile way, from the direction of the canyon's entrance.

"Tell me that's not what I think it is," said Julep, reining up beside Slocum, who had retrieved his brass telescoping spyglass from his saddlebags.

"Oh, if I told you that, I'd be lying." He handed her the spyglass. "See for yourself."

"It's Deke, all right. Riding out front like a big dog, just like he always wanted." She shook her head.

"And it looks like he got all the other things he wanted, too," said Slocum. "Like all his weaponry, and a whole lot of fresh recruits, too. But they're not moving all that fast. That gives us just enough time to head back to the Apache and try to convince the chief that I really wasn't lying. Maybe the sight on the horizon of an army advancing on him will do the trick. Come on!" He reined the Appaloosa around and sank heel.

He thundered onward a hundred yards or so when he glanced back—and saw Julep looking from him back toward her brother's increasing close-to-being-completed rebel army. She sat her horse still, and regarded him.

"Julep!" he shouted. "Come on! We don't have time to waste!" he said as he rode back to her side.

"I know, John . . . but he's my brother. They're nearly all my kin, for better or worse. I have to try to stop them. I have to try, John."

"Judging from what I've seen of them, you're on a fool's errand, Julep."

"Like yours?"

He sighed, then nodded in agreement. "You have a point, girl." Then he leaned forward and kissed her on the forehead. "I guess you have to do what you believe in your heart is the right thing."

She nodded, her eyes glassy with unbidden tears.

"Take care of yourself, Julep. You are one special lady."

"And you, John Slocum. It's been good to know you." She smiled "Look me up sometime."

"Heck," he said, giving her a two-fingered salute off his forehead. "I may just drop in when you least expect me, girl." He smiled and winked at her.

And without a look back, they each headed apart on their own separate fool's errands.

When Julep caught up with her brother's rebel army, she rode right to Deke, forcing him to rein up. He called a halt to his rolling arsenal, and the dust cloud slowly dissipated.

His excitement at seeing Julep alive was short-lived, since she came at him like a wildcat.

He tried to calm her down and, ignoring her questions, led her back toward the wagons. Smiling like a kid with a new toy, he tugged aside a heavy canvas tarpaulin to reveal a gleaming Gatling gun. "Them Apaches won't stand a chance, Julep! With all this gear, we'll surround them, then mow them down."

"But what about the women? The babies? The old ones? They never did anything harmful to you. What about them?"

"You gone savage on me, Julep?" Deke's confusion was evident with his knitted brows, though a slow-boil anger had begun to nudge its way onto his face.

"You need to stop this, Deke. Fighting another army is one thing, but slaughtering innocent people who just want to be left alone is plain wrong."

"I reckon not, Julep."

"Then you're more twisted than I thought you were." She turned to shout to the others, in an effort to convince Deke's followers that he was deranged, that they needed to stop this madness.

But she never got the chance, because Deke wrapped a big hand around her mouth and held her kicking body until Cooter got her tied up.

"It's for your own good, sister. I'll come back for you once we take care of them Indians, then you won't never have to worry about anyone bothering us in the canyon again."

"You can't do this!" she shouted, tied up and leaned against a rock. "You can't kill those innocent people." She continued to shout at the rebels as they marched on by, some on horseback, some on wagons, many on foot, all armed to the teeth and looking confused but ready for battle nonetheless.

Soon they passed her by and she sat sobbing between

shouts of pure rage. Her horse grazed patiently a dozen yards away. Finally, Julep began wondering what John Slocum would do—and she began to methodically work at the poorly knotted ropes that bound her hands and feet.

19

Slocum had made it halfway back across the plain when he saw a large cloud of dust, much greater than that kicked up by Deke's band of rebels. It looked like it was headed his way. Could it be more of Deke's recruits? If so, it would be impressive, indeed, and would prove Slocum wrong about Deke's powers of persuasion. It couldn't be the Apache; they didn't have horses enough to kick up dust clouds to choke a dog.

"Who in the heck?" He slowed his horse as he continued to ride toward it, and it toward him.

But the closer he drew, and the closer it drew to him, the more he began to recognize the sounds of a battle-equipped mass of men, began to see telltale signs of . . . blue uniforms, heard precise orders barked in English, and finally, he saw the unmistakable sight of a U.S. Army cavalry guidon snapping overhead just as he heard a bugle cutting through the dust and haze.

And off to his left, high up on a rise overlooking the long plain, he saw a small band of ragtag Apache, silently watching as two fierce forces slowly made their way toward each other. And joining them from the east came a rider. Slocum couldn't be sure, but at that distance, it looked to be the chief. Had he gone to the nearest outpost and tipped then off? Why now?

Slocum puzzled over this all as he rode northeastward, cutting a wide swath away from what was sure to be a battlefield soon. He headed toward the Apache contingent atop the far-off rise.

He reached them and rode up boldly. The chief nodded toward him, and he returned the gesture. Nothing more was said, but Slocum turned his attention to the battlefield. Now that he was sure the Apache were safe, he had to figure out if Julep was safe. The army's arrival changed everything.

Soon the battle began in earnest, and any thoughts Slocum had of the U.S. Army putting an immediate halt to Deke's army evaporated as hoofbeats, bugle blasts, and gunfire erupted. Slocum eyed the vicious collision from a distance with his spyglass. He could see no sign of Julep, and for that he was relieved. But where was she? Hopefully staying well back from harm's way.

The chief rode up beside Slocum, who regarded the man without showing suspicion.

"It was my wife who finally convinced me, John Slocum," said the chief, not looking at Slocum, but at the battle raging below. After a few more moments, he said, "She said that you are honorable and honest . . . even if she is not."

Slocum felt his face redden.

The chief continued. "She also knows that her husband would not back down from a fight, no matter how much might the enemy had."

"I'd say she's a wise woman, then, Chief."

"Perhaps. She also is . . . a handful."

Slocum was tempted to say "two handfuls," but he kept his mouth shut.

20

Neither man had an opportunity for more such talk, because the battle took a decided turn against the ragtag rebels. And that was when Slocum saw in the distance, but racing fast toward the battle, Julep, astride her horse, reins slapping the beast hard, first one side, then the other.

"Oh no—she'll be killed," said Slocum. Before he could kick his horse into action, two Apache men on horseback grabbed him on either side. He struggled, shouted, "But she will die!"

"Perhaps," said the chief, turning to face him. "But so would you in trying foolishly to stop her. You would never make it in time. But she will die as she chooses, with the truth in her heart. And with her brother. And that is better than dying angry and wrongheaded and alone, is it not? Living a long life, but with the knowledge that she could have helped him but chose not to, as he was massacred before her eyes?"

Slocum understood what the chief was saying, but still he struggled in vain against the iron grips of the warriors. Everything in him screamed to help her. Eventually he nodded, knowing that the chief spoke the truth.

"It is as she wished it to be," said the chief. "We spoke much last night, she and I, and we each helped the other to understand better our places in the world. Family, it seems, means as much to them"—he nodded toward the battlefield, and Slocum assumed he meant Deke's army—"as it does to the Apache." He thumbed himself in the chest.

In a few short minutes, the battle, except for random shots, appeared to be over. The U.S. Army had swarmed over, then ultimately trounced, Deke's poorly assembled ranks of ragtag rebels.

Slocum collapsed his brass spyglass and handed it to the chief. "For you. May you always see your enemies before they see you."

The chief handled the fine piece with care, admiring it, then tucked it inside his tunic. "I would wish the same of my friends."

Slocum nodded, appreciating the man's wise words.

"You are welcome to visit my people anytime, John Slocum." The chief leaned close and said, "But you will sleep far from my lodge." He smiled and reined his horse around toward their hidden home in the rocks.

Slocum suspected they would soon be moving.

As he rode northwestward, Slocum was overtaken by a cavalry soldier, who ordered him to stop. "My sergeant told me to question you, mister."

"Fire away, then." Slocum kept a hand loose, hovering near his Colt Navy, just in case.

"Do you have any idea where they came from, mister?"

"Who? Those crazy rebels?"

"Yes, sir, that's who I'm talking about." The army man seemed miffed with Slocum's answer.

He was about to mention the canyon, but something held the thought just on the tip of his tongue. Instead, he suppressed a smile. "No. No, I don't. I'd guess they were just passing through, looking for a better life out West."

"What about the Apache?" said the soldier.

"Oh, I expect they'll find a place to call home. They know this area well, after all. They've been living here peacefully for a long, long time."

"Frankly, mister, I don't know how anyone could live out here," said the soldier, reining his horse around. "It's so . . . unforgiving."

"To them, it's paradise," said Slocum. And with that, he touched his hatless forehead, reined his horse northwestward, and rode away.

Watch for

SLOCUM BURIED ALIVE

424th novel in the exciting SLOCUM series
from Jove

Coming in June!

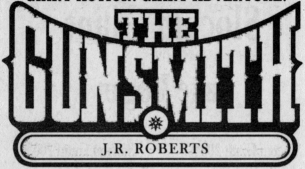

J.R. ROBERTS

M455AS0812

LONGARM

GIANT-SIZED ADVENTURE FROM AVENGING ANGEL LONGARM.

BY TABOR EVANS

penguin.com/actionwesterns

Jove Westerns put the "wild" back into the Wild West

LONGARM
by Tabor Evans

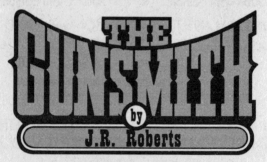

THE GUNSMITH
by J.R. Roberts

SLOCUM by
JAKE LOGAN

Don't miss these exciting, all-action series!

penguin.com/actionwesterns

M11G0610